GARNER

Garner

KIRSTIN ALLIO

COFFEE HOUSE PRESS

MINNEAPOLIS

2005

COPYRIGHT © 2005 Kirstin Allio
COVER & BOOK DESIGN Linda S. Koutsky
AUTHOR PHOTOGRAPH © Michael K. Allio

Coffee House Press books are available to the trade through our primary distributor, Consortium Book Sales & Distribution, 1045 Westgate Drive, Saint Paul, MN 55114. For personal orders, catalogs, or other information, write to: Coffee House Press, 27 North Fourth Street, Suite 400, Minneapolis, MN 55401.

Coffee House Press is a nonprofit literary publishing house. Support from private foundations, corporate giving programs, government programs, and generous individuals help make the publication of our books possible. We gratefully acknowledge their support in detail in the back of this book.

Good books are brewing at coffeehousepress.org

LIBRARY OF CONGRESS CATALOGING-IN-PUBLICATION DATA
Garner / Kristin Allio.

p. cm.

ISBN-13: 978-1-56689-175-2 (alk. paper)

ISBN-10: 1-56689-175-2 (alk. paper)

1. Women farmers—Crimes against—Fiction.

2. Summer resorts—Fiction.

3. New Hampshire—Fiction.

4. Family farms—Fiction.

5. Farm life—Fiction.

I. Title.

PS3601.L444G37 2005

813'.6—dc22   2005012569

SECOND EDITION | SECOND PRINTING

3 5 7 9 8 6 4 2

Printed in Canada

Thanks to many gracious readers, of many drafts. And to my husband, Michael, steadfast and incisive reader, with a sixth sense for story.

for Michael

Part One
The Postman

I

1925

The postman used the roads and the woods alike and bare-headed on a day that provided such weather. If he came upon Frances it was always she who saw him first and he who, knowing himself watched, was pleasantly startled. A tree became a girl, he allowed himself to wonder.

Today, the stream was full with a sudden rain after a dry spell but he was a man of all weathers. Perhaps this was how he came to be postman. He dressed for modesty and economy in the same layers June and January. In spring the mud was clean and deep so as could heal a wound and if the postman had ever put his mouth to a gash in a maple tree and sucked the sap he told no one.

At the edge he held a sapling for balance, put a hand in, dabbed his forehead.

At first he thought it was an odd reflection from a reddish leaf, or a brick-colored stone on the bottom. Then he leaned in closer and it was surely blood for it curled and sank through the water. He thought to himself, it's one of those thin-skinned summer boarders who's gone and torn the hook out and then thrown the fish back in the water. It was only that much blood, as would come from a fish's mouth, but it was strange, he could smell it. Too rich for fish blood. It was mammal. Once he caught the scent it clung to the back of his throat like sulphur. He tried to clear his throat of the viscous sweetness. Cloying, like the smell of a dead animal lodged where he'd insulated with horse hair and some sawdust beneath the cold floor of the bedroom.

The postman lifted his eyes across the stream half expecting to catch a cowed fisherman in city attire and ill-fitting boots borrowed from Frances's father. Instead he saw Frances. "Hello!" he called before he could stop himself. She floated on her back, her undergown swept aimlessly about her. Her long hair was unwoven, the light green of willow wands through the water. Where had she left her clothes, then?

He felt the way he always felt when he saw her. Braced himself against the sapling, a prickling like the little sharp hairs when his wife shaved the back of his neck in the kitchen.

The curtains of the forest would be tightly drawn and then suddenly she would issue forth, throwing the green gauze wide, not the least bit bashful. He would crash forward as if to catch her at her new game and however she might explain herself would delight him. She might say, "Why Mr. Heald, you've caught me bathing. A bath in live water has countless benefits." And she would break off, as if distracted by the very air itself, fragments of light and shadow.

The forest rang as if he'd hurled a stone instead of spoken. He broke off a dead branch for the crack it provided. There. A hand in the water revived him.

It was ice cold. She might have frozen before she drowned. Too cold for the season from all the rain. He drew his hand out quickly. A man must not presume to share her bath. I must say a prayer. For the girl Frances who would consider a stream fine as this one succor enough for soul and body.

⁓᛬•᛬⁓

The postman did not speak during dinner. He thought to make up for his misplaced greeting in the forest. Mrs. Heald kept her gaze on her plate until she could stand it no longer. She rose abruptly.

After dinner, as was the habit, Mrs. Heald reached for her collage-making box and the scissors and paste she stowed on the mantelpiece. Willard Heald used his dark sleeve to brush salt from the table.

"Will you pass me a bit of the newspaper." He broke the silence. Mrs. Heald withdrew a sheet from beneath her project.

Sometimes his wife had cut out headlines or drawings to include in her collages, and then Willard leaned over to see what had interested her. If she added a scrap of fabric, a round wooden button, dried flowers, it was a haphazard quilt, and he became irked and remarked how would she store it?

An act of leisure—but he fought his own disingenuousness for her sake. At least it was handwork. Besides, he had his own habit.

There was a hole in the paper his wife passed him the shape of a young woman in a long dress. Willard cringed, then let out a huff at himself as he read the print below—

A modern bride may wear a traditional gown. He allowed a glance at Mrs. Heald's work in progress. Indeed, a stiff cone of lace had taken her fancy.

He took a pencil from his vest pocket. He had thought to compose an obituary but began instead, in the margin of the newspaper,

> From the daily threading of the woodland
> roads I am privy to the long slow cycles.

History has faded into nowadays, thought the postman. Rich farmland is built upon by strangers, an entire orchard goes a second year unpruned, no apples, humpbacked stone walls crisscross forests that were once handhewn pasture.

Trunks knuckled like a working man or woman. Lost ladder left for a year. Unconscionable waste. A lightning scar goes unmended. Old dog licks at the charcoal groove. Death awaits him.

> For the sake of new commerce, an orchard
> is gouged out and graded. An old woman
> comes to Town Meeting and cannot be convinced that the town did not lose any
> acreage by losing a hill.

War memorials are observed with gunshots over the graveyard and the volunteer Fire Department hosts a baked bean supper. In the tight breasts of boys and girls, thought Willard Heald, loyalty begins to shiver. Garner's officer of the peace takes his place on parade and the last day of August is the last day of summer and the concord grapes on the road are green as virginity and matted with dust and birdscat and some hasty animal vomits them up in the goldenrod and aster.

> Locals fish in streams carved through deepest woods an ice age ago. Beaver Brook and Blood Brook and tributaries of the Saskoba. They weave their lines through potato bugs, entrails of crow's eye blue and gleaming red.
>
> A girl drowns in their fishing hole.

Mrs. Heald reached over the dining room table and put her hand over her husband's hand. "Read it aloud, will you."

On other evenings such a signal from his wife would mark his finest hour. Indeed he often found himself spinning out the town's history or he would illustrate family trees with exquisitely rendered leaves and local birds perched upon their branches. He could draw maps to scale barely glancing at the paper. He laced the town roads with his own footpaths through woods and field—as the crow flies, shortcuts. But his wife's voice was different tonight. The sudden death of a girl had provoked her. Well he had told her what he saw. A girl dead by drowning. He had not mentioned the blood for it came from no wound he could discern—and how he had thought he had her simple company alone in the forest.

"Bounded by her trees was the new England," read Willard without pause. "It is said that if one had the gossamer soul of an angel and wings of an artist's weave, one might pass from Maine to Rhode Island, crown to green crown, and o'er New Hampshire.

"Such are the White Pines of New Hampshire. Straight as masts, full skirted as a woman.

"Tree to tree, one might travel."

He had heard them called the hardwood gentry—oak and maple.

"But the White Pine, privilege of kings, friend of settlers—there was no better contender for emblem of New Hampshire."

He paused and felt more keenly his wife's eyes upon him. Well he would give her this then, the fact that he had in his possession a letter that Frances had written.
"Perhaps this is how Frances came to set down on a loose sheet of letter paper, *Lay me as if in some small animal's burrow, buried in needles and duff, beneath the White Pine. For there is no one from whom I take more comfort.*"

(Once Willard Heald said to his wife that he felt he must do the best he could for Frances, that he was her guardian angel and when his wife snapped, "I see no well-loomed wings, Willard," he nodded gravely and offered,
("Humans may be angels where angels can't be found."
(Frances was the first person he knew closely who was born in the Twentieth Century.)

"How did you come to read her letters?" said Mrs. Heald thinly.

"Almost every day she managed to detain me, Mrs. Heald," said the postman with a certain affect. "Of course she spilled the contents.

"She sent inquiries to a nunnery, and she wrote to the great American novelist Winston Churchill who himself has always fancied New Hampshire."

Mrs. Heald kept her hands busy as her husband spoke as if to deny the conversation.

"A wise and solitary heart," proclaimed the postman.

"Solitary," echoed his wife, although it couldn't be said she meant a challenge.

("Mr. Heald," called Frances. Her voice seemed to him lush for a girl, sonorous and demanding, vibrato on the horizon like before a thunder. But she had a girlish habit of making odd couplets of conversation.

("I've so few possessions. I could directly partake of the nuns' lessons."

(The postman craned his neck to see from where between the maple leaves she was speaking.

("Just this heart-shaped pendant"—Heald caught sight of her hand darting birdlike as if to drink from the cup at the throat of her throat—"and a Letter Writer's Kit from my cousin in Manchester.")

(He thought it was ten years ago he had delivered a maple box of writing paper. Folk were accustomed to retrieve their parcels at the post office, which was no more than an alcove of Buck Herman's store Heald used to quarter the town—roughly—and sort the letters. But he had taken it home with him, the package, since they were neighbors. Her composure was a rare thing; neither shy nor high-strung like a filly or a rabbit. Now here is a child who will hold her own against the Century, had thought the postman.)

"Willard," his wife broke in. "You've stopped reading.

⊰•⊱

Dear Mr. Churchill, wrote Frances. *I am a woman of the age to decide what pursuit I must take for life. Marriage is out of the question as I have always been ill at ease with those of Adam's*— and here she stopped and sat a long time with a still pen at the desk she borrowed from her father, cocking her head this way and that into the dark corners of the study. How was it that she wanted perhaps to become a writer and yet she dared not use the word sex, which, admittedly, had been the first word to come to her mind, and the second word she thought of was race, but in truth they were not a different race altogether—and so she began again.

Dear Mr. Churchill, I wish to become a writer. What advice can you give to a fellow American, a woman approaching the age to choose but born and bred in a town smaller than your thumbnail, tucked between merely knuckle-sized hills?

Isabel was a school friend who had already secured a place in a nunnery. She sat upon the wooden steps of the library (it had been a schoolhouse in the postman's time) and read to Frances from Greek mythology. The postman crossed and heard Frances cry, "Give us Persephone!"

He thought such an association beneath her.

Isabel called the afternoons idylls. "You're a ghostly girl," she prattled intimately.

"Will you write to me from Malden?" said Frances.

Isabel stopped oddly with her neck jutting forward.

Isabel said that the vows she would take at the nunnery were a safeguard against the corruption of adulthood. I will not take adulthood, he heard Frances chant softly. I will forswear the modern world, Willard added as if for his record.

"Indeed, Mrs. Heald, are you listening or absorbed in *collaging*." He made a remark of it.

"For in that time," he continued, regardless of her permission, "children were born who were more old-fashioned than their parents."

("Do you mean our time, Willard?" she had inquired when he read the same passage on another occasion.

("Ah, Mrs. Heald," he stalled and she continued.

("You see us already set into place like so many gravestones. Are we so soon finished?"

("Not finished, but to remain as we are. Constant against Time in our Moral Nature.")

"Such children," he resumed after a pause she thought gave him ample satisfaction, "were the acolytes of the past and they became spinsters and hermits. They were born this way because it was the beginning of a new Century and because of a world stripped of whimsy and because, simply, they abhorred the thought of growing older."

Dear Isabel, wrote Frances. *I have come late to the cross-roads. I must now make a choice. You have preceded me because of your angelic nature; what shall I do? Write to me of the practical life of the nunnery. Have you achieved anything in prayer? Isabel, I am greatly confused. It seems my father will take in boarders from New York City for the summer. I am to serve their meals and make their beds. They will pay five dollars a week, a portion of which will go into a bank account for me. What if some of the young men make advances?*

In the postman's mind's eye was the erudite author's particular penmanship. *An address to a young woman called Frances because the women of America have more of the future in their hands collectively than any other group of people in the world.*

"A noble thing for him to say," said Willard quietly, or in a voice that seemed to his wife oddly thick.

She might have asked how he knew such a detail but she bowed her head to continue her handwork.

❧•❧

In the evenings, Frances's father and brothers talked over the new planning Ordinances. Willard Heald recorded such conversations.

Our town is no longer somebody's kitchen garden, the selectmen said, and the postman recorded this also. We must plan for growth. As with a child, our town needs a strong hand to guide it. Now a farmer could not do two things unless he told the town planning board. The exception was syrupping. But beekeepers would be taxed. Three or more fruit trees of a kind would be recorded. Extra cream was to be called surplus.

The new Ordinances are for the birds, said Frances's father. We'll build where we please. We'll not count our apple trees.

Russet
Russet
Mac
O'Connor

A daughter in a nunnery. Now is that a loss or a gain for the household? What do the selectmen say?

Frances's brother Wright snorted.

I won't marry, said Frances.

Pine board additions may be made to the original structure if they are approved in advance by the planning board, wrote Heald the postman.

> Sugar maples may be tapped in the earliest spring regardless of property lines. Wool-cards and bobbins (the latter by the factory-folk) can be made from any maple, but save your sugar for its sap. Men come from the sugar house covered in sticky film that any good dog will lick at if you let him.

If someone wants to make syrup, he is a more virtuous man than you but despite your lassitude, your children will be treated to maple syrup on snow at the first possible occasion.

> The fiddleheads of certain ferns may be col-
> lected by the children and had for a light
> supper. Native cuisine, as native as winter-
> green berries, Indian cucumbers, the green
> layer of black birch bark in spring.

Chewing the bark, you could eat winter. Set your teeth against its ache, thought Willard.

> Red Oak for shingles. The last of the Balm
> of Gilead sighted on the west ledge of the
> Jewett Farm.

> The Ordinances said that blue skies were cus-
> tomary but work could be done as well when
> skies were gray. Trees were meant to be leafed
> and green but in Garner there were nine
> months out of the year when they were bare.

The summer boarders were mostly young men who felt very free to make advances. Garner folk hold their tongues, and, as if a June thunder, wait for insult to pass over.

> Every house must be situated on at least
> one-half acre of land and centrally, so that it
> would not be too close to the road. A
> proper plot with a proper house and prefer-
> ably a fence around it is required.

> The town of Garner is shaped like a sail.

A sail-shaped shroud brought from some attic. A girl so light—one man alone could carry her to her father.

> There shall be no living in old railroad cars
> or other discarded motor vehicles.
>
> Scrap shacks and bearded men living as her-
> mits—you may be ejected from your farm
> for back taxes.

And yet the tax collector or the selectmen or the sec-
retary or the town planner or the surveyor or the librarian shall not tell you when to pay your taxes. There is no
notice you receive by mail. It is like intuition or the
weather. Scores of people owe back taxes.

Willard Heald himself had never cared for hunting,
but hunters, he granted, must be allowed to hunt in
apple orchards in all seasons and negro apple pickers
must be exempt from the stares that otherwise accumu-
late around such a person and eventually drive him to a
larger and more southerly city.

> The Revolutionaries left us their motto.
> Live Free or Die for the men and women of
> New Hampshire.

A dog on a leash belongs to a sissy. If a woman cries
when her husband is signaled off the road for misde-
meanor, the officer is not allowed to write out a ticket.

Massachusetts is a different country. Vermont is for
deviants. The state of Maine warrants a cold respect. The
rest of America is of no real consideration.

White Pine should be the State Tree. Mountain Laurel
the state flower. The lady's slipper is a rare woodland

flower that grows alone. A woman who can make jam from wild strawberries will never be a spinster.

The best wives must go to the selectmen and volunteer firemen. All other men will get the second pick.

Religion is at once social and silent.

A true lithium spring is one in which the lithium occurs naturally in the spring water.

Women shall travel in pairs until they are married. Women can be anything they want as long as they are wives. Men can be anything they want as long as they can fix their own machines. The best man is a kind of gentleman mechanic.

A good hand with animals must be well regarded.

Not every man is to be expected to know how to shear his sheep. The sheep-shearer must be kept in business.

> The Ordinances are such that protect the
> locals of this town and preserve its integrity as
> the only inland sail-shaped town in America.

Willard Heald gazed past his wife into the dark that had surprised them both: this new autumn dusk like homemade felt that muted them so early.

For some of our native folk, to meet the modern age was a difficult task. It was I who came upon young Frances, face up in Blood Brook and floating. I left her there and went for her father.

Her bare legs were pale blue as if her blood had frozen inside. He lifted her head with his hand. Her eyes were closed. Willard Heald thought, I knew she was a girl with good sense to close her eyes in dying. Then the postman's stomach emptied out and he sat down hard on the bank of the stream in pine needles. In his mind's eye he summoned his verdict—how one of the summer boarders had stolen into her bedroom in the night and he knew too well how she had lain there stone cold—landlocked, he thought, as Garner—and how she had alighted through the forest singing under her breath, "Let it be known that this will always be my home, let it be known that this will always be my home," for the woods still carried the echo.

"A girl drowns in Garner," he continued reading as if he had not met his wife's eye. "A girl drowns to escape the modern world. We shall hold fast to our own. The peccant future shall not taint her."

II

Frances's middle brother James, good with his hands, sawed the legs off an old bench and made it into a swing. "A perfect place for our idylls!" called Isabel, who made herself quite at home anywhere. Frances, slim and straight as a reed, edged around the porch carefully with a tea tray. Isabel had already gathered her feet beneath her.

"Tea?" said Frances. Her mother's old set, limp yellow roses seeping through the hairline cracks. When she finished her cup she customarily turned it over to read the script on the bottom. Each time it held meaning. Each time it seemed more reticent than the last so that she worried that in time the secrets of all old things would be lost.

Frances settled herself beside her companion. She kept her feet on the porch so she could rock the swing just slightly, to lull Isabel into telling her a story. "Will you tell the one concerning Persephone?" she said shyly.

"Oh do," she repeated, gaining confidence.

"Let me see your hands, Frances. A clever man can always tell by the lines in a girl's hands," said Isabel. Frances extended her left hand, holding tightly to her teacup with her right. Isabel smoothed the palm with the back of her nails, traced a line the breadth of it. "A girl with fleshy or unlined hands is a trickster," said Isabel. "But yours are wrinkled like a virgin."

Isabel became suddenly pensive of late and then impatient, flustered without warning. Another of Frances's brothers (there were three: Wright, James, and Joseph) appeared around the corner. Isabel dropped her airs and leaned in to Frances, hissing, "Does he know I'll go to the convent, Francie?"

It was Isabel's damning whisper: "Persephone"; the abduction from a bewitching forest, that brought a hot blush to Frances's face. She was dry brush for kindling, her very breath threatened ignition. She would go next time, she promised herself, to one of the Town Hall square dances. She would tear across the whole floor, the Town Hall would catch on fire. Why was she never in this state on a night when the dances were actually transpiring?

And then it always came to her. She must not ignite. She would go to the woods, for in her woods there was no danger. White Pine, soft and still for ages.

⤙•⤚

The summer boarders came by train to Maynard or Saskoba Falls and Frances's father hired the boy Asa Robinson to collect them in the boy's father's automobile.

Frances's father was a lean and horse-gray man who played the organ with great sympathy. The boarders were immediately delighted with his exacting country style and offered to pay him extra for his organ recitals in the evenings. Frances was directed to collect the money. In her long-boned, tidy hands she extended a china dish.

Frances still had not made her choice. She prayed for Isabel's welcoming letter to reach her, and she studied

Mr. Churchill's correspondence often at night. *A woman who writes may choose not to marry. Have you read the Emilys? Dickinson? Brontë?*

Frances waited for something to speak to her heart. She took long walks when she was not needed at housework. Sometimes she met Heald the postman. She liked the way he nodded to her—full of a grave intent, as she thought only a grown woman could inspire.

At first, her mother said how lovely for Frances to have the company of the boarders and she pulled Frances playfully outside by the apron and they cut lilac and a branch from the crabapple tree. But soon Frances's mother tired of the way the young men and their women who were "cousins" or "friends' sisters" lingered over tea in the dining room (she saw the flasks whisked from pockets), then stayed downstairs late, and hollered to each other when they finally did quit the common area and retire.

At the end of the day Frances's mother regarded her hands like bristle brushes or flannel rags, tools separate from her body. "You might buy these at the Hardware," she said. "The feet too." Frances dragged a low stool across the floor with her foot and her mother drifted down like leaves. There was just the dish of coins on the table—the dish Frances passed as her father thundered and wheezed at the organ.

Of late she placed herself straight as a saw-milled board upon her bed but could not sleep. She cringed recalling the things the boarders said despite the presence of their fashionable female cousins. The one north window in her little room was a dark eye. She was not safe here but her heart surged.

She knew the delicate floral pattern of the inside of the china dish. Different than when she washed up with her mother, poached halfway to the elbows by wash water just off the stove. Their fingers became pink, bloated, almost obscene. The dishes were like river stones only they might break at any moment and then her mother would rush to the rescue, too late. Two pieces in two hands.

It was unreasonable to imagine he was at the door but she dreaded it just the same. The curiosity she had for the city man's smell of cedar chips and mothy lavender might have crushed her.

Tonight, when she held her hand toward him, eyes lowered to watch again the pattern of violets and wait for the hot clatter of coins against china, she felt the shock of his touch as if she were a water creature returned, suddenly, to water. Just her wrist, slender, but it might have been the plunge of her innards.

He didn't grab it like the man who sold corn feed in Westborough, like her brothers sometimes grabbed it to pull her out of a daydream, but he figured round it with the pad of an alabaster thumb. As if he were following a singlet of ivy, flowering vetch, and he marked gently where the roots went in.

She had not dared to look around. Down each long finger he went. The dish sounded off the crash of four sleek half dollars. It was too much, she knew. He hadn't meant it for her father—for his skill or for the upkeep of the organ.

When the century has bent down and
folded its neck for the swan song, someone
might happen across a china dish and
remark upon its delicately painted violets.

Names dug in birch bark and a footpath and
a fallen penknife might be forgotten, but for
our townswomen, the china dish remains.

—*From the predictions of Willard Heald*

She mostly haunted Abbott Road but there she was
floating just ahead of him around the corner on a track
that veered off Hunter's Hill and led to a poor clapboard
in a hardscrabble clearing fast yielding to sumac, milkweed, ash saplings. It was called Poor Farm in days when
Garner might have also been called a community,
thought the postman bitterly.

Frances turned around for a second and he nodded.
"What business have you here?" he said when he caught
up to her.

"Oh, I've no business. Only come to wonder. There
was talk it would be vacated. Where would they go, the
Poor Farm Millers?"

"That's a fair question indeed, Frances. Where does
anyone go, who leaves us?"

Frances hesitated, looked past the postman down the
track that was the road as if it might tell her.

"People are not meant to move about so," said Heald. "How should I know where to deliver their mail?" He feigned laughter, or tossed it toward her and saw she caught it and made an examination.

"I don't know why they shouldn't go if they want to."

A dusty dog came trotting down the lane sent out by Helen Miller. Frances crouched down immediately and called to it.

"Mr. Heald," she said ponderously. "Will you ask for me. When you deliver the letter. Will you ask where they'll be going?"

He was so often caught off guard by this girl. He was light-headed. Was it she who followed him about and sprung from the trees or the weeds unannounced and curious? Or was he following her as if spellbound? Did he know, in fact, the way he knew that Helen Miller's letter was an invitation from an old and bitter friend to help with a shoe shop in Keene, that Frances would be here awaiting him?

It had most likely been a month since he was at the Miller's. He hurried toward the carved-out homestead. The dog stayed behind with Frances.

"Of course, Frances. They're going nowhere," said the postman, when he returned, almost boasting.

"Indeed!" Frances exclaimed. "To live out one's whole life between the same horizons—for shame.

"I shan't stay long, although I love my forests."

Heald called out to her but she was already gone through the forest.

There was gaiety in the voice that came lilting between foliage and shadow. "I'll waste no more time on the Miller's!"

Then Heald's mailbag was a bag of stones on the ground beside him.

No, he would say to her. Next time, as it struck her fancy to appear and disappear. Stay, he would say to her.

There was no rustle left in the woods when he put his mailbag across his shoulders.

⊰ III ⊱

The Puritan township was mandated at six miles square. Those who came first claimed hilltop sitings, but homesteads must be to some degree clustered for protection.

What good was a neighbor if he failed to hear the stentorian bark of the dog you'd made to sleep against your farthest fold? thought Willard.

From the start a man could earn his plot by the bounty placed on any manner of wolf or wildcat.

Moose were measured from earth to shoulder—fifteen hundred pounds—and seven feet.

A man was oft reimbursed for the tract he sowed with English grass. It was the sun more than the oxen one must harness and drive forward.

There might be depraved wilderness between the townships: New Hampshire, or Mariana as was its earliest appellation, was like a patchwork quilt missing odd pieces, as groups and individuals would apply for particular acreage and other acreage—the beaver ponds and lowlands—would be left out. He thought of his wife's collages. Those undivided, unnamed tracts of land among townships were awkward and of irregular boundary. They were known as slips, or gores, as in a circle skirt. To the Puritans who had crossed from England on great ships stocked with cases of limes against scurvy, the slips looked like shrouds or sails.

Sail-shaped edges of land.

Of White Pine and Laurel.

> The town was known first as Sliptown.
> Then as Maynard Slip, for the township of
> which it was an ungainly sliver.

Samuel Blanchard would be married. The girl's mother required her to write to her aunt in England that there would be a wedding and any extra supplies would be well-received. We are pioneer women of a sort, the girl's mother dictated.

No, we are Puritans.

Samuel Blanchard was the surveyor from the town of Westborough. Garner was the private thorn lodged in his side. Just the thought of it. His tools:

Axes
Flintlocks
A Brass Theodolite
Wooden Tripod.

He told his new wife on their wedding night that the compass needle varied with locality. They couldn't have children—the doctor in Boston confirmed the peculiar arrangement of those parts inside her. He did not touch her anymore for fear of feeling her organs in lumps and bulbs.

When she was quiet at his side Samuel Blanchard thought about the iron chains he carried through the woods. The unclaimed woods of Sliptown whose trees took on the shadows of hostile ancestors at sundown. In these woods he felt like he had lost his right hand. Loggers and woodchoppers with lice in their beards and rats in their bellies poached at the edges.

Where was England when he needed her, the Queen's lawn, deer parks with artfully placed oaks?

His chains were four rods in length. If he used a hemp line instead—well, it was lighter but it shrank in damp weather.

The surveyor from Maynard added a man's arm length to every chain to compensate for uneven ground.

Samuel Blanchard's wife was the nomenclator: there were few persons of education in such a frontier and she was called to devise other titles as well. Not all roads could be called the King's Road, not all valleys the Valley of the King.

She wore a gold wedding band studded with three blood garnets, for which our Sliptown was named. On the day of the naming, early November, Garner was a town with a population of thirty-odd souls. Militia men came from Westborough and Maynard and marched from the banks of the Saskoba River half a mile due north and the track they made was called, with optimism, Main Street.

In that year and many others, the stream named Blood Brook was nearly all frozen over.

—From the studies of a humble postman

❧•☙

Frances's father would not have a funeral. He moved a spare cot to his shop and laid her there, wrapped in heavy wool blankets. One by one the summer boarders drifted off, some in the night without paying, some with a raised eyebrow and scarce words to their host.

Giddens's long face was plaster and the features greased on like a clown in a circus. He looked past his guests, into the gray evening.

He was a man ahead of his time—too much grieved for a child dying. Frances's father had reserved a great gentleness for his only daughter. She was born late in his life and his expectations he had already exhausted upon his sons. He offered his daughter free reign over the new Century. He thought that the world should appear for her as feather-light and whimsical as he imagined she was herself.

He was not a man to lay blame without certainty. Or accuse, as would befit murder. No, he could better imagine his only daughter dispersing like ground fog, or a season.

It seemed to his sons that his capacity for grief overbore any anger. He had said to them before—as children—that nature knew no righteousness.

For three days the shop stank worse than rats caught between the walls in winter. The smell curled under the door and yellowed the tongues of all the family so they found work to do in the farthest fields.

Finally the eldest son, Wright, spoke to his father. "We'll be sick if you don't bury her." He was not a crude young man, he was as finely reared as Frances, but neither was he afraid of working with his hands. "I will arrange her burial with the money from her china dish."

The father awoke as if he had been struck hard across the mouth. He wiped his lips with his hand gingerly then and said, "No. The money from her china dish was to be her future. We will bury her ourselves but commission a headstone. I want a tribute," he stumbled.

Wright Giddens was charged to go to the mason who could carve words across the polished shoulders of granite. He poured the coins into a pouch. The coins would not have fit in his pocket. He considered their heft, what they could buy. A new steel saw blade. A prize lamb from Eben Temple whose ewes bore twins weighing more each one than another farmer's singleton. The lace curtains the schoolteacher coveted and screens for her windows.

His eyes grew small. He didn't think that death was frivolous. He did not know if he believed in the spirit. Sun, soil, and water. He believed in his hands. He looked toward the buxom middle of the century. He began to sweat. Prosperity.

The smell of death was on his clothes. The mason took the pouch of money.

It is New Year's morning in 1776, Willard Heald imagined. The town has been named and then lost its name in the wake of a Revolution. In the evenings, people count their belongings. Women sew pockets along the inside seams of coats and bodices. There they hide the things that are precious and perhaps no longer loyalist.

A heart-shaped pendant.

A quill pen for the daughter who had wanted to keep her thoughts.

A box of writing paper tucks under the bed.

Garner is a slip of land, sail-shaped, now disclaimed by any one of its three neighbors. These neighbors themselves are not sure if they exist, to what rule they belong. Maynard to the west, Westborough north and east, Saskoba Falls still with its thundering wilderness. In Maynard Slip, as the tract of land is called again after it is deemed too small and awkward to be called Garner, only three families have settled and stayed. None are Tory, all have lost infants and children. All will send their remaining sons to fight the British. Together they will send ten bushels of rye to Boston after trade with England has ceased.

—From the records of a postman

There is a girl we shall also call Frances, although she is not our Frances. She has a brother. He will go too. He is Elliot, Ethan Elliot. He has what they call a rooster in his pants. Once he gave his sister Frances a peacock feather and she stuck it in her hat and their mother clapped her hands, delighted, as Frances paraded by. Their mother's hands were covered with flour when she clapped them and flour covered her bosom. This was the moment when Frances realized that she loved her mother.

It is New Year's morning in 1776. The selectmen of three towns and a representative from the Slip are gathered in someone's stable. When the men stomp their feet against the cold, the smell of hay rises and they think of other seasons and the fishing they will do in Beaver Brook and Blood Brook and the tributaries of the Saskoba. Someone says this land will be the new England.

Ethan Elliot has a rooster in his pants crowing at dawn and a mane around his neck that he can't help shaking. In the length of his strides he feels he could have all the women in the world. His father is a selectman. His father has brought him here to someone's stable.

Flaxman from the Slip has called the meeting. Snow is in the air. We must test our neighbors to find out in their souls if they are the true sons and daughters of this Revolution, says Flaxman.

What Revolution? We are already free, says Ethan Elliot the firebrand.

His father kicks him hard across the shins. His father would take an axe to his testicles if he couldn't hold his temperament, he said.

Ethan Elliot is thinking of his sister. Frances with gray in her hair already. At eighteen, pewter strands. Frances with hands like snow and brows like feathers. If only he could find a wife like Frances. No, a wife won't quiet him down as his mother has promised. No, love will make him wilder and stronger and better and he will beat his chest in the morning and break often into song.

Paul Smith is soft. He mimics young Elliot, "What Revolution?" he pitches his voice high even though Ethan Elliot has a deep and sound bass. "Watch your boy, there, Elliot," he says. "Here we're all of one mind."

> The selectmen instruct each other to strike
> the shins and exile by popular force all those
> who refuse to sign the Association Test.
> Dissenters shall carry a brand. All sign.

Ethan Elliot is afraid of battle. He is not afraid of love, but he has not yet found it. From the road he sees a girl with a long feather in her hat. In his heart a sudden ruckus; and then a bittersweet falling begins and as the heart falls it catches on all the stock furnishings of hope for the future that even a man so young has already gathered. In his memory he sees this girl with her hands in the stream, they have been walking, and they cut off the road and stop at the stream—she is up to the elbows, her face pitched to the sky, the weave of branches above them. He cannot distinguish her voice from the voices of the birds in this memory. Then he sees this girl from behind, standing in their mother's kitchen, and she does not know he is there and she is telling her mother some gossip.

He feels his heart snag against her bird-like laughter.

—*So dreamt Willard Heald*

1788. Mariana, Lands of Masonian Proprietors, finally New Hampshire, belongs to the rule of the United States of America. A spinster at thirty says in her soft voice that she cares not for cream on her berries. No, no, she murmurs, a girl gone gray at eighteen has no right to a husband nor to cream on her berries. It seems her voice has been taken from her and mixed with equal parts of air and water.

1790. Garner is a station for the new Post Riders.

1791. The young spinster finds an old love letter in the family Bible. The paper is as yellow as her skin and through it she can see the shadows of her veins a greenish blue. It is signed by her brother who died in the war.

To read it is an arduous and hollowing task.

Initially, most of the settlers to New Hampshire want hilltop homesteads. There the view is the finest, the streams have their origins, and one can watch the stranger approaching. The wind is strong in the winter, but the settlers and their wives plant windbreaks of White Pine or erect their barns and outbuildings to the north of the farmhouse.

Between 1776 and 1795 sixty new roads are built in Garner.

By 1800 fifteen of the roads have washed back into forest and seven are redirected.

1797.   A bass viol for the church! It is voted who will board the musician once he may be located and who will organize lessons for a few of the children.

1800.   Vocations include Fence-Viewers, one, Wood-Corders, one, Culler-of-Staves, one, and one Sealer-of-Leather.

—W. Heald's history of Garner

⇥ IV ⇤

Willard Heald heard everything with his ears made of envelopes. He could go prowling about a farm as if he were a thief. He had a slice of blueberry pie at the school or the store or the fire station. He stood in the corner and ate the pie, coffee if the stove had been stoked, and the corner of any room took him in like he was its kind.

Heald knew that no wood or stone or (by God even) iron barrier defined a town so surely as the correspondence its citizens sent and received. No surveyor's maps in drawers at the Town Office could so exactly delineate. Yet there were places in the wall punched through or tunneled under. He alone knew their coordinates, and kept them secret. For instance:

Frances Rebecca Giddens
Giddens Farm
Abbott Road

The return address was a powerful scrawl although a woman's hand—not a country woman. One of those contemptible summer boarders, Malin Nillsen, New York City.

Isabel Killam
Killam Farm
Four Corners

The return address, a neat hand, but smirking, J.S., Boston.

Only Heald knew that Isabel did not go to the nunnery in Malden, Massachusetts. Having been quite compromised by the same, she was lucky indeed to elope with Jack Sawyer, bank man from Boston.

These correspondences were the threat that Willard Heald stubbed out as he wore a deep groove where he trod that might fill in with the spring snow melt.

Even nimble Frances should find the borders impassable.

-ᢖ•ᢖ-

"I do confess to you, Mr. Heald," called Frances from her usual woodland perch. "There's a gentleman who quite fancies me from my father's gang of rascals.

"He's gone quite out of his way to find me here and there.

"Do you really think they are scoundrels then, Mr. Heald?

"And why shall I be afraid of them when I'll be a nun next year!

"Or a writer, there's that too. Have I another letter by chance from the estimable Winston Churchill?

"Oh no," she laughed. "Don't come any closer, Mr. Heald. This is my tree and I should hate to share it.

"And what of my companion Isabel Killam? I suppose she has no time for writing. I shall have to post her another plea. Patience is a virtue, Mr. Heald, especially when there are so few virtues to choose from in this modern day."

Her laugh of green and silver. Laugh of leaves.

"What part do you play, then, Mr. Heald?"

Willard took a step back, caught his heel in a root, stumbled to keep from falling. "Tell me, Mr. Heald," she continued daringly, or sparkling, "had you always wished to be a postman, and even as a young boy?"

Now the postman found his voice. "My dear Frances," he said. "How is it that you know this gentleman, your father's boarder, has indeed taken a fancy to you?"

> In this first quarter of a new Century there were children born who were more old-fashioned than their parents and attuned to the weather and by whose lives sacrifices would be made to secure history, said the Ordinances.

—*W.H., Ordinances*

All at once Frances dropped from her branch and fled through the forest. When Heald bent to pick up his mailbag, he caught a glimpse—like a white-tailed deer or a silver fish in silver water.

Mrs. Heald said, "It won't do any more to keep her letters to Isabel. It won't help her learn the ways of men."

"And women," broke in Willard.

His wife pushed herself out from the table. "I'll leave you to your writing then. But what will you do if she really does go to Malden?"

"You have such fancies."

Inside Mrs. Heald a rage began to form against her mild-mannered husband, against Isabel Killam, against Frances herself for keeping to the forest. For assuming that the world would come to her in Willard Heald's mailbag. For allowing herself to be flattered by a rakish swine from New York City for pig he must be to take her wrist and not her hand as Willard had reported.

Once upon a time Mrs. Heald had had a girlhood companion—for a girl must have a companion in Garner. The roads were too dark to walk alone and the fields were filled with rocks to twist an ankle and a girl would be left for wolves or travelers. Mrs. Heald, long ago called Columbine Mason, found her best friend in Sarah Leary. She remembered her Sarah with giddiness like salivating before a green apple or a wedge of lemon scantily sugared by her thrifty mother. Once Willard had asked her if, despite all that had happened later, she'd like to set down some memories of Sarah on paper. He offered to take her dictation, or just to talk so as to help in her thinking. No, she had brusquely declined and gone off to clean up dinner.

They lay side by side in her father's fields and named the clouds the names they hoped for their children. They took fresh bread to the schoolteacher on a Sunday and found him crying over the death of his sweetheart in Connecticut. She remembered how Sarah had cast her a brave glance before she went over and put her hand upon the schoolteacher's shoulder. She, Columbine, had mastered a deep ache in her throat and gone out to draw him a bucket of water. Later, they'd cried for him together and Sarah's mother stood puzzled in the doorway and said, You live in a world of your own and I shall never understand you.

They did needlework and knitting for each other's hope chests. Willard had never asked her, but she'd understood that after what finally happened to Sarah, it would be unsuitable to keep the lovely things Sarah had made for the Heald's marriage. Well, there was one handkerchief that Mrs. Heald kept—but it had a stain in the corner and would have been condescending to assume the poor could use it. Willard always said money didn't provide aesthetic taste and she took it to heart and only offered her finest things to charity.

Sarah met Harry Maury at the store and was gone in a fortnight. He was on his way to California and he asked her to marry him quick and to join him. Sarah had looked round at her prospects: Why, we're at least a dozen men short! she declared. She was something of a natural actress.

Along with the stained handkerchief, Mrs. Heald still kept the letter she received some three years after her best friend's departure. She never drew it out anymore— the cedar chest was like a coffin. But she had read it often enough so that it was no longer Sarah's voice she heard as narrator of the letter but her own.

My Beloved Columbine Flower,

Here is what has happened to me in the place called California. Save this account and, when your own Daughters come of age, require that they read it. It will trouble you some for you were always more delicate than I but know that even still I strive to be noble.

We know nothing of Men but what our hearts tell us and our hearts are those of virgins who think that as we bestow care so will care come to us through our Husbands. Perhaps your own life has shown you this.

Some day when I am old and free I shall set out to find you. Remind me then to recount our journey from New Hampshire westward. There are an abundance of lively stories and I thought the beginning of my knowledge of Indians and other Species. But for now, my dear old Companion, I have means enough only— both in soul and in currency—to tell you of the thing that has befallen me and the way I make my livelihood.

We found ourselves in the land of California in time for me to bear my child in the home of Pioneers who were good Christians. I trust you have done or are near the same, my Columbine, and so I'll not report it. My Husband and I were blessed with little Knight Maury. I stayed on with the Pioneers through some weeks of convalescence while my Husband traveled with new-found friends to find an even more frontier county. I shall make this short so you shan't have to trouble yourself much in your consideration and evaluation of my choices. I would never be allowed to return to your company now so what is the value of your disapproval?

My Husband shortly wrote me to say he had made us divorced in the eyes of the law and there was no God so how could He possess eyes to view a marriage or not? Stay with the Pioneers, he advised, then ended his letter by asking me to send Knight to find him when the boy had money to bear his old Father. I felt I heard his laugh along with it. Soon, finding that I was a Divorced Woman, men began to court me in their singular way: a night here and a night there. Your Daughters shall know, Columbine, that I made a union with all of them. When I found myself with child again, I did not take the poison that the Pioneer Doctor advised me. I stayed on at the kind house where I was with Knight on my back and soon Stephen, the baby, to my breast and worked in the kitchen we had set up there for travelers.

But these details of frontier life must mean little to you. I ask you now with some bitterness: would you let my Sons marry your Daughters twenty years into the future? For daughters I'm sure you shall bear.

Then, when Stephen was past danger of the early infant ailments and Knight spoke his first sentences, I took up my children and left that place. There were no trinkets or keepsakes stowed in my baggage, only the names I had kept of fifty men who might have been my youngest's Father.

Are you shocked, my Childhood Companion? But I am at work for the rights of womankind. I make my living from man to man and each one thinks he is the Father of my most glorious Baby. I am paid handsomely to be a mother. We travel by rail and coach—my feet do not touch the ground except to cross their dooryards.

Willard had given her the letter. She passed it to him when she had finished and she stood quite ashen and cold in the full sun of the doorstep.

He granted her a solemn pause. She wouldn't have known that he didn't need to study the letter. "It is a great tragedy," he said. Then, as if to comfort her, he said, "We shall not have daughters."

They sat at the table again and when dinner was cleared and Mrs. Heald had done the small things that are the anchors of one's life—feeding and sheltering—she set up her collage-making and Willard drew out his pencil.

She knew he was writing about the death of Frances Giddens. She had come across a discarded paragraph: "What Might Have Unfolded," and it had irked her intensely that her husband should imagine the fortune of another woman's life. She recalled herself, not one week into marriage, laying out the contents of her hope chest on the unfamiliar double bed. Would she wish such a moment on the girl Frances? When unfolded, her dreams looked like dish towels and pillow shams and runners and doilies.

Some minutes passed in silence and Mrs. Heald was not in the frame of mind to attend her collage. She glanced at a letter in the local paper from a neighbor, that was odd, she remarked under her breath, Franklin Abbott. He is a man of the fewest words, she thought to herself, and she recalled how Margaret White Abbott had run off with a soldier leaving her husband and young son to the kind of indigence that descends upon a farm without a woman. There were ladies who found no love in Garner, thought Mrs. Heald. Margaret White Abbott, her own Sarah Leary, Isabel Killam. But do they find love elsewhere? she wondered. Mrs. Heald recalled that when Margaret was pregnant with the boy she hired herself off to be photographed as a specimen for a biology book published only in Boston. Even for her husband Mrs. Heald had never stood naked.

Mrs. Heald read the piece without holding the paper, not wanting her husband to notice it till she had finished. *To the editor*, wrote Franklin Abbott.

We must look more carefully to the death of the girl. My boy gave her lessons once. She was a strong swimmer. My boy will testimony to her hardy swimming style. The male guests from the city who might have led her there for a joke or worse should be brought to question.

Our own townsfolk too. Some were closer to her than others. Has anyone seen something amiss, I ask? The girl was fond of our forests.

Sir, in my life I have learned that there are times when God looks elsewhere. It is then that we must act most righteously in our duties.

"Willard," Mrs. Heald spoke more sharply than she had intended. "You've nearly been called to task by our very own neighbor. Have you not read what's beneath your nose?"

"I have, Mrs. Heald."

"So what do you say? How did you go about your route all day? How did you deliver mail to Franklin Abbott?"

"Franklin Abbott does not receive mail," Willard said with finality. He went back to his writing so that to interrupt him would have been as hard as catching an owl's eye in his own forest.

"Do you think Frances would have liked to know how we were heroes in the Civil War?" Heald said after a time and without looking up.

"Willard!" Her voice was shrill.

"A grave note; a note to the grave, Mrs. Heald."

"Is such meant for humor?"

He caught himself.

Seeing him bent then she bent too—if not a touch, a shadowing of his posture. To recall tenderness she thought of the way he mouthed the words as he read over his verses. A low voice he wasn't aware of.

It is 1860 and President Lincoln demands seven hundred and eighty men from New Hampshire. They will serve for a period of three months. Town Meeting is held in Garner to see how many will go up to Concord.

Our boys have names the undertaker already knows and his assistant, the engraver, has made note of. They are Edmund, Oliver, Alvah, Isaac who enlisted twice, Isaiah, Joseph, Abraham, George, James, and Martin who has a wife. Their names are in their family Bibles. Leather-bound family Bibles on bedside tables in gaslit farm-houses in Garner. They assemble in Concord. There is cheering, the passersby call out. Fathers go up with their boys. Edmund and Oliver's father is red in the face, a flask. Alvah is a slim boy. He asks if he might try one of

Oliver's smokes. From then on he is never seen without one. His hands shake.

> Then President Lincoln calls for one thou-
> sand forty-six men from New Hampshire.
> They will serve for three years. They assem-
> ble in Portsmouth.

These boys also have names. George and Wilbur and Joseph and Thomas and William. Charles Felt, the only musician. Their names are less fanciful than the names of the boys who went first. These are the boys who didn't go on a whim or for a truth. These are the boys who hold their mothers longer and tighter than they should. Whose fathers don't go to Portsmouth with them. We should have enlisted first, they mutter to each other. Those others will be home two years and nine months before us. Imagine if we only had three months, they say to each other.

And yet at the Battle of Bull Run it is the New Hampshire men who are the first to fight and the last to retreat, heads held high. They can walk faster than Massachusetts, the Green Mountain Boys, Maine, Connecticut, even Pennsylvania. They are made of granite. A different stock from those in the southern states. The soil is too rich, and boneless. It is because they have not done their own work. There are no stones in their streams, either. Life is soft even at its edges.

> 1863. Garner has its first town Christmas
> tree, forty feet high and staked at
> the north end of Main Street. It is
> not lighted, for this is wartime.

1865.   Nelly Killam renames her six-
        month old son Abraham. Her hus-
        band, the one-armed Joseph Killam,
        is not offended by her allegiance to
        another man.

What Martin who loves his wife remembers when he
is dying is that her skin is like lace. This is the highest
praise of beauty he can think of. How when he presses on
his wife's breast just so hard a spangling of red stars
comes out, no they are rose, or magenta. Then a nurse
comes into view from one side and tells him he has
already been dead for half an hour.

1867.   Russia says we have enough cold land
        already, take Alaska to your breast. A
        ladies committee makes Alaska
        ornaments for the decoration of the
        town Christmas tree. What other
        tree than the White Pine. The
        wooden letters A-L-A-S-K-A turned
        on a bicycle lathe. Quilted husky
        dogs and sleds. Snowflakes made
        from a variety of media, including
        tiny snowflake cakes, scraps of news-
        paper, the ribbons of wood that curl
        from the lathe. There is a banner
        made from an old tablecloth of Nelly
        Killam's: Welcome to the Union.

1884.   Article 4: to see if the property tax
        rate should be raised to $16 per

$1000 and who would do the assessing.

1888.   The third wave of French Canadians comes down for the mill in Saskoba.

1891. $80 in taxes collected for the licensing of dogs. Such money as if raised shall be allotted to the upkeep of the Old North Cemetery.

1895.   The first telephone from here to Saskoba Falls installed in the formal parlor of Mrs. Albertine Joslin.

1896. $5.65 is reported for the overnight boarding of tramps and a similar sum for defense against gypsies.

—Collected by W.H., some from dreams

(Mrs. Heald thinks it odd that her husband does not write from his own life. Where are your good parents in Garner's history? Your own wife?)

❦ VI ❦

Plowmakers before John Deere:

Fish
Tuttle
Wyatt
Weston

You needed a smithy to make a plow. To hire it out—
well, you would be an assembler rather than a plow-
maker. In Garner, you couldn't afford Whiting's rates. In
a way you would've liked to have paid him just to be near
him—a preacher and a shrewd man of business both. It
was common knowledge that last year, 1810, his
preacher's salary was five hundred and as a blacksmith
add one hundred fifty to that. He kept sheep and he made
his own charcoal for the smithy. Another seventy-five.

At night, at your wife's bidding, you prayed to the
whim of the Lord. If there were specific things you
needed, Whiting's commission for a new plow, your
wife's mother's illness to subside, you bid your imagination rise in a column of pleasantries and promises from
the bed where you lay. When you were rendered otherwise speechless by the bare innocence of your youngest,
who asked how to pray, you said crudely, "Send your
thoughts upward."

Whiting knows:

Make a cot for the watch
for charcoal, as for syrup or lambing.
Ten cords of wood stacked high and tight,
the dog begs to sleep by its master.
Does the woman shed her garments
in the same fashion when you
are gone and does she
dream of girlhood?
The boy's job in the morning:
cover the wood with wet leaves
thick cuts of sod
bales of weeds dampened
with a bucket of water.
The boy's job at midday:
cut a hole in the top—by ladder—
drop the flame
down the center.
Keep watch, boy, till supper.
The dog noses around,
smells fire,
brackish smoke,
a long, slow smolder.

Between the blacksmith and the tanner:
a heavy horsehide for the making of an
apron, a quarter-dollar plus a nail in a
horseshoe for barter.

If the charcoal-making catches fire, send for the boys
from the nearest schoolhouse. Twenty boys let loose
from schoolhouse No. 5. Their sleeping dogs leap from
the bushes, biting the schoolteacher's heels. The whole
pack singing in unison; witness to such a blaze.

At night, the preacher Whiting prays to God from his watch cot. His charcoal costs more, for it is both dense and flinty.

—*W.H., research and reflection*

❧•❧

Once Frances is allowed to watch the charcoal.

"You'll get the better of us, Frances. A woman who can make charcoal in the Twentieth Century!" Her father is proud of such an experiment. He envies the man who will marry her. It's not that his own wife isn't a hard worker.

Her brother, Wright, is begrudging, even if he doesn't want to do it. He's to go with Peter Whiting to a farm auction in a town dangerously close to Boston. For prices, that is, a dangerous bet, a waste at best.

You make a hole in the top of the snug cordwood insulated with strips of sod and cold weeds. The fire breathes all night. Be careful. Frances's brother is impatient. If there's a blaze, will she sleep through it? It will be his fault if there's an accident. He thinks he should know how she sleeps, Damnit.

But he has never passed the night with a woman.

After supper, Frances makes up the cot with old tablecloths her mother saves for the purpose of night watches. A blanket, September. One of Isabel's brothers drives Isabel by at dusk just to see. Two raisin biscuits in a muslin sack. The farewell is stage-whispered.

"Good-bye." And, "You're a strange bird, Frances." Frances notices for the tenth time that Isabel has exquisite feet. Ankles that are not indigenous to Garner.

The charcoal-making must be far enough away from the house and barn that should a fire start—the dog whines, smoke in its eyes, its throat. "No," Frances says, and then wishes she hadn't heard her own small voice.

She dreams the pile glows red hot like an iron in the fire. She dreams her father comes through the field and the dog rushes at him, barking and snapping. What is the matter? The dog so spooked by the dark? What happened to your nose, dog? Frances sits up and the cot sags beneath her. Where is the dog? No longer beside her. She whistles for it. No answer, no rushing through the hay as if you had paws of wind, dog. Instead, someone else's mercury steps. Loose hay kicked up as the figure comes toward her.

❧•❧

He came upon the girl Frances sitting discreetly on a stone wall just off the road. Had he been traveling by automobile or even carriage, he would have missed her. But going by foot, one felt the breath of the shadows.
    Or, the scratch of her pencil.
    Even her breathing.

And then a small rock fell out of place and Frances gave a tiny laugh of tinsel and green to be discovered by her friend the postman.

> We have stone walls that were built to last
> for ages.

Stone walls that cross the laws of Ordinance when no man nor road may endeavor to, stone walls that will leave a ghost weight across the chest of the land even when, in so many hundreds of years hence, they have been hauled off or washed away, thought Willard.

> Our stone walls rose out of the earth by the
> hard hands of fathers, mothers, here and
> there scampered the children. The fathers
> cut the trees with axes. The ring of the axe
> and the creak of the trunk as it bent to a
> crash muffled by an upperworld of leaves
> that wilted in a matter of hours.
>
> The mothers made piles of the wood, and
> the children set fire to the branches.

Green smoke for five counties, Willard imagined. The fathers and the neighbors dug the squat trunks out of the ground and burned these too. Now there was a field where a forest had been. From this new field the families and the neighbors hulled granite and piled the stones into walls upon which Frances might perch.

"Frances," he called. "Will you go to the square dance this evening? Here I am about to deliver your invitation."

"On no, not me," Frances called back through the leaves of the forest. "I haven't the stomach for socials."

"What will you do then, sit on the stone wall till supper?"

For a moment Willard could not tell if it was Frances laughing or the forest playing some trick on his ears that were, for the better part of each day, unaccustomed to human laughter. Then Frances called gaily, "Why you're even more solemn than I, Mr. Heald. Perhaps I shall go dancing alone by moonlight!"

> The people cleared the land and the sun shone upon the new pasture and grass grew that could feed a farmer's livestock through a winter. Orchard grass and Timothy were planted. Scythed in June and again in September.
>
> Stone walls were the labored script of the country man in that century. And yet one could climb Hunter's Hill or for the ambitious of leg Monadnock and far down below the stone walls appeared to be the nimble and common cousin of the mountain goat.
>
> —*Recollections of a small-town postman*

"Frances could have been a beautiful girl had she chosen to cast her smile upon us. Instead she seemed to appear only in corners of rooms or walking on the road with her head severely lowered. But when our paths crossed—I on my delivery route, she on some errand for her father or simply out walking—she would respond to my greeting with a clear voice that might have come from the very sparkle of sunlight.

"Hers was a voice that caused one to whistle upon parting.

"'Have you a letter for me, Mr. Heald?' she called across the road.

"Only once she received a letter from a Mr. Winston Churchill. 'A suitor?' I said.

"'Heaven, no,' she, looking up abruptly. I feared for a moment I would lose her good company, but she saw I meant no harm and went on. 'I have no suitors, but this, I hope,' and she held up the letter with all the brightness of unsullied youth in her eyes, 'is from a mentor and a guide. Good afternoon, Mr. Heald.'"

> Residents and summer folk are united in their appreciation of our common countryside: even its fickle weather—or is it meretricious?, its children who learn from birth to cull rocks from the tilled soil. Bowers of apple blooms in spring and the old-fashioned lilac, the peaceful wending roads that were once marked from tree to tree, one-horse pathways into dragged roads that lead from neighbor to neighbor and between the open doors of friends and fellow citizens.

"It was with pure intentions, I believe, that Frances's father wished to share his home with the summer boarders. They came with fine references and bestowed upon all a lively if not worldly air," read Willard.

> And yet, while our sunsets are something for such visitors or more southern-hearted sentimentalists,

for those true sons and daughters of Garner, those with the bones for the early morning, tools in hand, those with bones like beams on which the woodworker has carved a compass rose, those who scoff at loneliness and some are fishermen and some are farmers and some are the owners of your local grocery and postmen and stonewall builders and a girl called Frances—for them there is the sunrise.

—*Simply, W.H.*

"There were three young men who came to board at the farmstead on Abbott Road that summer. Jaunty fellows all, in wit if not in body, caring not for the country life on principle but for mild distraction." Willard paced the kitchen like an actor upon his stage.

"They were not so far in age from Frances, and there were those who whispered that the girl's father, a clever fellow, was setting the stage for an engagement. I knew better: Frances herself would never allow it.

"I soon heard that the city boys thought our Frances plain at best, sober, dour, and sometimes rude. I would have rushed to her defense, begged to differ with the dapper youths, for I considered the quiet girl a friend and saw the light of imagination in her eyes. But my wise and gentle wife put a firm hand on my own hand and nodded in her way that meant I was to leave the young folk alone.

"So I quieted myself and let the banter continue."

In 1905 there are ninety-one farmers in the town of Garner.

In 1905 Albert Fish purchases the first butter maker with a cream separator.

In 1908 A.F. purchases the first hayloader. In this year Frances is born.

In 1915 A.F. votes against a tax increase on farm machinery. "We're still men of sweat and blood," he declares hotly in Town Meeting.

Our folk are disinclined to keep farming into the new Century. In families such as Giddens there is some rancor. Late at night the men are still talking.

We will let go the low wet field that borders Heald. We will take summer boarders, says Frances's father.

Frances's brother curses strongly, perhaps too strongly for the occasion. When you are gone it will be my land, Father. Then I will have to start from scratch picking rocks and clearing fields. I can't entertain city people in the summer and for weekend sleigh rides like you. I am no sad country clown.

The debate in town is over taxation of farmland. Should rates be raised or lowered to encourage production? Giddens makes a living off his land also, Temple points out, who has bartered his tax in curly-headed Romneys; just not in corn or apples. Without the land there would be no boarders.

There is a Town Meeting and Grace Weston Derbyshire serves refreshments. Records are kept and she will be compensated for lemons and sugar, a batch of butter biscuits.

> Article 11: to see what should be done about an automobile left on Main Street overnight. Is it necessary to draft an Ordinance? The street sweeper is Asa Robinson who gets his scant allowance bimonthly. Buck Herman is in possession of these records. Asa Robinson, please stand and state your case. Let it be known that Garner is not some careless municipality. A curfew is not necessary if we all use decorum.

A farmer must don another hat, says Frances's father. Leave the straw with its sun-shielding brim in the field. Mice will make a fine nest of it. A go-ahead man cannot be a farmer. Our hardpan and granite is no competition for the black earth of the new West.

Apples, Father. Look at Barry, McCloud, even Greene. Sugarbush is a sideline! The rock maple grove that grew for free. Dairy! Poultry: forget our poor soil!

How are my children more old-fashioned than I? says Frances's father.

We have a farm, replies the brother.

Folk want respite from the new urban life. Wholesome food set up by the women of the house, a cleansing dip in our streamwater; I have a daughter, thinks Frances's father.

Albert Fish is the first year-round Garner resident to buy an automobile. It has not been forgotten how in 1907 the mayor of Lexington, Massachusetts came up in his new horseless carriage and it turned over on him and his wife was forced to raise the thing and at once extract her husband from underneath with her umbrella that she had not brought for this purpose.

Wives extracting husbands with their umbrellas, chuckles Frances's father.

1919.   Interment of the five brave Great War dead shall be in the West Cemetery all but for Carroll Weston, the fourth Weston son, whose body was lost at sea.

In memory of Carroll Weston who earned three bronze stars. Garner grammar school. Tewksboro County high school. Married Aimee Ritchie at Newport, Rhode Island. Would have made a fine addition to the crew on Good Roads Day.

—Penned by Willard Heald of Garner

Heald at the kitchen door with his dripping hat, his fogged glasses. He has been appointed to a committee that will plant a tree in the West Cemetery in honor of Carroll Weston. Selectmen of Garner and trustees of trust funds have allocated exactly the right amount of money. Less would buy a seedling instead of a sapling. More would be draining a coffer already run low for the sake of foreign soil.

Heald had passed the cemetery on his way home and there was Carroll Weston's mother Elinor kneeling at the headstone of her father. Rain filled the crown of her hat. Another son's black overcoat clung to her straight back.

Mrs. Heald keeps the kitchen warm in any weather. There's a news item she's left out for him on the table: Population of Garner, not including workers for the Saskoba mill or summer residents: 1799—945, 1849—689, 1915—201.

"Why, does that mean no one has counted in five years?" he cries into the empty house.

Willard Heald had meant to say to Elinor Weston, Your son died in the war to end all wars. He meant to say, Come out of the rain.

> To be held at the First Congregational Church, Garner, a rousing welcome for the boys who returned home on Tuesday in time for their mothers' suppers! Spruce yourselves up to honor our native American soldiers! Fifty-five dollars has gone for a marching band with a fanfare at seven o'clock. And, Ye shall be fed, Townspeople!

> Interment and the commemorate planting
> of a hardwood sapling will take place in the
> West Cemetery for Garner's war dead.
> Saturday ten in the morning.

Heald pushes the newspaper aside. Then he had crossed paths with the girl Frances. "I'm waiting for Mrs. Weston," she whispered.

A slip of a girl. Less hardy than a mayflower. He could not tell—was she ten years old yet? Twelve?

"You'll catch it in this cold," Heald had said sullenly. Why did he feel she had already been watching him? Saw him pass Elinor Weston without proffering his coat or a single obliging sentence?

"I'll offer her some comfort, is all. Do you know she's been wandering the graveyard for some hours?"

"One of her daughters will be along soon, I suspect."

"I've a bit of brandy in a flask for her. For when she passes this way."

The postman had started. Of course Frances's father would know a bootlegger. They were a dime a dozen even in Garner; but that the girl should speak so freely.

Heald sinks to the kitchen chair placed there long ago to keep his wife company when they found there would be no children. That the girl should speak so freely to him. She must have a heart the size of a bird's heart inside such a narrow breast. Of course, it would be a year till Prohibition took effect, but there was the Lever Act that he himself supported with an unwarranted passion—grain was for feed or bread, stomachs not heads, indeed there were hungry soldiers in wartime.

He is afraid of her. She climbs trees like a boy but her arms are thin as needles. Once a cloud of flower petals came down upon his head. Her face was the tiniest seed pearl from high above him. Her laughter was sprinkled almost tenderly.

"Mr. Heald," she had called. "Do tell me what it was like on your wedding day!"

He had closed his eyes. She tilted her face to the side and he swore her features were brushed on—so lightly—as if with a feather.

> News item: Eight Garner boys are attending high school this year.
>
> Dr. Hanniford Joslin will commence construction of a concrete dam across the brook in his front yard.
>
> Appeals to the library committee must be countered by Friday.
>
> The Special Aid has voted to contribute at least ten cents each to the French orphanage fund.

Garner's only woman to serve in the Great War, Emmeline Tobey, returned from Saratoga, NY yesterday where she was a decorated nurse.

Three cheers to you, Emmie. From the boys.

1925. There are nineteen farmers left in Garner and Frances's brothers are not among them. Frances's father plays the organ on summer evenings for the boarders.

Winston Churchill writes, Marry if you can.

Isabel does not write.

The girl Frances takes to the woods that are, in places, so dark and dense one feels to be inside one's very own shadow.

—*A layman's history, by W. Heald of New Hampshire*

Part Two
The Summer Boarder

I

Midcentury

Old North Cemetery

As if evening itself were a chimera, I part the drapes to see whether the streetlights have come on. Turning back upon the darkened parlor is like turning inward, I have long felt. A dovetailed maple box sits in considerable repose atop its own marble pillar. Hollow chest and heart in hand, I spread the photographs out as tarot cards, for I live alone and indulge in a spinster's pleasures.

Or, my guests cry, Malin, won't you take out your old photos of New Hampshire? And I oblige, my famous half-smile projecting its false mystery. I am in possession of rather a grand old Fifth Avenue apartment through the wealth of my father, and the display of this homely talisman surprises my visitors. I have had lovers from whom I took less comfort.

Take this photograph, the apple orchard beyond the graveyard. There were tunnels between the trees through which we ambled, green tunnels. I wanted very much to taste an apple. Frances goaded me and laughed when I puckered. "They'll not be ripened till the end of September."

One was surprised to come upon a graveyard in the midst of a verdant orchard. I drew my breath in superstition and Frances fairly chortled. "Don't be afraid of my ancestors, Miss Nillsen." It was here I first laid out my proposition. We would have a kind of exchange, I suggested. Frances would return to New York with me at the end of the summer season and I would accompany her back to Garner for what I called prettily, the Original Thanksgiving. "You would despise the winter," she argued.

"Now you're discrediting *my* ancestors," I said.

Why didn't I just take my picture of the orchard without its shadowed alcove of headstones? Four maples took the corners. Footstones for the very long or the very wealthy, said Frances, eyes laughing.

"Your apples, Miss Nillsen, will be all in cider by Thanksgiving."

Does every young girl born on the edge of the twentieth century want to become a writer? I certainly did; and when Frances confided her dream to me I felt a jealous tug as if she had already succeeded by the declaration. She had a capacity for solitude that even I, the only child of a self-made man and without a mother, had to envy. She possessed the kind of narrow view of the world that is a gift in this day and age when one loses an intimacy to breadth of experience. But I was still determined to be a cosmopolitaine, put up a parasol in every country.

The way a child derives a sense of herself, a true confidence, in the presence of her mother, so Frances's self-knowledge seemed to come from the backdrop of her precious Garner forests.

The box had been a letter writer's kit given her by a cousin. She said she had long depleted the stationery

with which it had come stocked and perhaps I could pro-
cure some more such fine paper in the city. I took it to
signify a promise we would write each other but it was
my folly: from me Frances needed nothing.

They've all their hands wrapped around the same stem—hayfork or hoe, I've forgotten. It's Mr. Giddens in the middle with neighbors flanking, although it was the one with full white beard like a bottlebrush I wanted to capture. Now there was a chore Frances confided in me she hated: the scrubbing out of a whole shelf of milk bottles. "Or the residue shall sour and give all the guests a stomach," she said.

Haying Is Not Quaint

I had always thought it to be—some light and delicious gathering of meadow grasses. Oh, like a fragrant prairie salad with minimal dust. How I was mistaken! To see the men's hands crosshatched with splintrous cuts just from haying! I had Mr. Giddens stand with the same neighbors and one of the hay carts just to show off the stone wall at this particular juncture. Frances corrects me: "Hay is a crop like any other. Meadows are for poets who have never set foot in New Hampshire."

Dare I say we had become inseparable? It was what I longed for. I had never met a girl who was wise as an old man and as unflinching. She came and went as she pleased and there was no explanation. "What do you do all day, Frances?"

"Rid the forest of its shivers. Wait on a letter. Haying is not quaint, Miss Nillsen. The country life is not for dreamers."

Plow Horses

Mr. Giddens had sold his off, but a neighbor arrived with a sturdy team and they did well when the terrain was steep or marshy. I strove to capture their magnificent straining chests and shoulders, the ribs just showing at the sides, the crust in their coats and the way the man driving them was greatly diminished. He wore a cap of black wool even in summer and in the photo his forearms show up knotted with sinew and ligament.

There was an evening not long ago my guests concluded that Garner was a fantasy. Of course we all wish we could go back to our summer of youth in the country, they sympathized. A place so impervious to time passing must eventually be passed by time, out of existence, said a certain gentleman with mock philosophy—I had once jilted him. But look, another guest had whispered to me upon his arrival, his recent wife is twenty years younger than the rest of us.

Here is a picture of the lot of us in our broad youth. Robert Yates in the center, his head of fire. It was bread and cheese and the tonic lithium water we made a spread of. Perhaps a jar of cider jelly from the previous fall's harvest.

Congregationalists

Here are the Garner folk gathered for worship. The religion of the Puritans shall always pervade, although by generation rather than coercion. I asked Frances, Does it bother anyone that your family does not pray on Sundays?

"Work is respected before God, Miss Nillsen."

There you can make out a little boy twined around his mother's arm like grapevine or poison ivy. I remember him specially. Deep-set eyes peering from a dense Colonial forest. I always say to my guests, "I don't suppose he got away, did he."

I might have sold this one to the town itself for documentation or tourism. I've an uncanny good eye for perspective. The street seems to go on and on and there's not a storefront I've missed on one side or the other. My guests always parry: "Why haven't you gone back? Bought a summer cottage?"

I admit to concealing the fact from my guests that I have never had a letter answered. Once I even requested a meeting with the Postmaster General, Borough of Manhattan. Is the mail up and working in this corner of New Hampshire? Has New England seceded from the Union? I asked cheekily.

Robert Yates, who called the place a graveyard, would be pleased to know I imagine my letters drifting about like large snowflakes in the Old North Cemetery.

Even after Frances declined my invitations to visit New York, I thought to return for Thanksgiving. I fancied I had taken her under my wing.

It was an afternoon I greatly looked forward to when, having cleared the day of further engagements, I went through my photographs and chose the ones I would send back to my hosts along with a letter enquiring about the November visit. I sent three—not to be strident. The first was simply of the house as the guest approaches. One can become overly sentimental gazing into a photograph. Life appears to stand still by one's own power and here I was the Maker with Garner rubbed off in black and white and taking up no more than five inches square of my inkblot. I thought for sure the place would only be more enchanting in the early winter.

Second was my portrait of Frances Rebecca Giddens. The background is the tree that was planted in the yard at her birth. "Who planted it?" I asked.

"Why it was the postman of course, who plants trees for all the children of Garner."

I thought long and hard to select the final photo for my little triptych. Should it be the one that so cleverly shows each and every storefront? A rather artistic view of the road winding away from Garner? Nature in all its potency where Blood and Sawyer Brooks converge to make a waterfall? The whole Giddens family arranged in the parlor? Finally I decided upon a simple record of the first frame house built in Garner. I inscribed it, as

Frances had impeccably related it to me, "The Whit C. Miller house, c. 1780. First frame house to go up in Garner; later a tavern, an inn, a school for the area children of the Universalists, and now the home of Ch. and Mary Jewett who have three children." Ah, I thought, Frances will be quite proud of her pupil in history.

I did not hear back from the family Giddens. I could imagine Frances somehow too light-footed to bother, but Mrs. Giddens? The closest I had ever come to having a mother? Wright Giddens, with his unflagging head for business? I contacted Robert Yates by letter, and waited through Christmas. Carl Adler had gone to Baltimore. I telephoned good old "Geoffy," although in truth I had been relieved to cut myself off from those people. "I don't suppose you know, then," said Geoffrey. "Something unfortunate with the Giddens family. We were forced to leave a week early . . ." and here he faded off and offered instead to meet me someday for a drink at his local. I was forced to decline, of course, as I have never put faith in his kind of gossip.

A portrait of Mr. and Mrs. Heald, he being the general postmaster and sorrowful busybody of Garner. Not a face you would remember—featureless, or stone-colored, or stone-shaped. But don't you think there's a flicker to his eyes as if he's memorizing the city girl with the photo apparatus?

I said, "Frances Giddens betrayed the secret of your lovely name, Mrs. Heald."

"Fanciful," she replied, but pleased that someone should take an interest.

Her husband looked away, embarrassed.

"So Frances is taking you into her confidence," said Mrs. Columbine Heald, warming. "She's a special girl, but not unusual for Garner."

"She'll make a fine lady writer for sure," I blurted.

"Is that so?" Mrs. Heald looked toward her husband.

"To be a good citizen is enough work for any woman," he said.

The photo had already been taken. I had nothing to lose by staying although the man had offended me. "According to our postman," said Mrs. Heald, "Frances Giddens is the one who keeps our trees so nicely. Do you know what she would write of, Miss Nillsen?" Without waiting for my answer she good-dayed me with a curt nod and left her ill-tempered husband to break off the session.

He did so clumsily and I nearly felt sorry for the country oaf. I think it was not my beauty but my carriage and propriety. He shuffled over his farewell so that I could barely hear him.

You can see the whole of the lower vegetable garden in this picture: all thirty rows of it. Mrs. Giddens said to Frances and me, "A garden is a church of sorts, girls," and I blushed from the chest up to be addressed like a daughter.

"Are you very religious, Mrs. Giddens?"

"Not at all." Her opening face had closed again and I regretted the question.

Frances, the daughter by blood, came to her rescue. "Lettuces and green beans are the common pew holders. They never last for more than a day and there's no point to preserve them."

Did I laugh politely?

"Peppers and pickles are the fold who hold the congregation with their doubt and their questioning. It's days and days we spend to can them, boiled lids sucked tight upon our green tomatoes. Cabbage, beets, and onions can last till January in a proper cellar and enough sawdust, or the old way with apples swaddled in cornhusk, but the only ones the church may rely on completely are those who are dead and buried in the plot next door. That would be the potatoes and the carrots."

It was a metaphor not without its bumps and switches but I was a convert upon digging my first potato, for I had not imagined the dun-hued staple of stews and leaden Garner breakfasts could inspire such sympathy. A brown bundle, I cried in childlike surprise. It was attached so precariously to its gentle greenery one felt a certain pang; I was a remorseful intruder as I unnested it from its white root, its garden cradle.

The Eldest Brother Wright Giddens

He might have stepped off the *Mayflower* last Saturday. I had never seen such a square face and silent of all expression. Here was a mouth had defied temptation. Gray eyes had never seen the gray ocean. But it was blasphemy to imagine him in any act of loving and his brow was certainly untroubled by that sort of emotion. (That Robert admired him alone of all Garner natives was something I might have taken note of.)

Yates was, of course, the closest I ever had to a betrothed and so I've kept his picture. We never spoke again after I returned to the city. What does such a man, to whom Malin Nillsen might have been married, look like? Was he the dashingest lad of them all? He was fleet of face—you couldn't have pinned upon him a single expression—and his humor changed by the moment. He had the high forehead of a wise child but because his hair was red and his complexion gingery people did not immediately trust him. But too simple to call him a fox, for he had the weakness, human, of thin-skinned men much loved by their mothers: he was deeply riled—no, undone—by female beauty.

It was the day I was to depart, earlier than the others, for my father had telegrammed to say that he missed me terribly and our dear aunt had passed away at eighty and would I return for the funeral. I thought to take Frances with us for one last picnic on that morning and I meant it to be a real invitation; that she was one of our equals and not some native tour guide. It broke my heart that she still called me Miss Nillsen. Truthfully, I had fallen out with the others by that time and so I rather depended on her company.

I should say it was really our favorite pastime, picnicking, and one you can only indulge in on a holiday. Frances betrayed that she thought it an awfully strange compulsion but she agreed to come along for the hike of it.

What a fine day it was; we set out all together. My trunk had been packed and carried off by the local valet Asa Robinson the day before—I had acquired only some native attire, like a costume, in Garner and had rid myself of some other dresses so the luggage was light as a feather. I felt in a strange way that I might drift off as well, inconsequentially, chaff of the grain, not essential. In my room I'd left only the small valise I came with. Mrs. Giddens would pack me some fare for the train and I'd take it in a hardware sack and give it to a beggar in Boston, just mortified enough by the grease-stained paper.

Robert was surprised to see Frances. "On our last picnic together, Malin?" he said with a nod in her direction. He made a great show of taking my arm and walking me slowly round the first bend in the road after which we'd come to our opening in the forest. What was Frances to do but surge ahead; no one else made any gesture of conversation.

I was furious and how I longed to break off our engagement. I wore no ring but I wrung my hands and shook them as if to be rid of one. I wanted to rush ahead and join Frances. She had a way of darting through the forest, sure of foot, and I had just recently found that if I followed heedless, not minding roots and bracken, my eye on her head in light and in shadow, I too could fly through the forest. But there was Robert's hook at my elbow.

She met us at the Poor Farm, recently deserted. She had plucked a salad from the wild garden and brought it round in her apron, urging us to add it to our bread sandwiches. I watched in envy: a natural Diana.

She stumbled in front of Robert, and he reached out for her most ably. He can always be counted on as a gentleman, I thought. I held my hand to her also, but she took Robert's and I noticed that her eyes were shining.

It was not, I thought, the least bit unkind when I chided her, "A schoolgirl attachment! You two shall behave yourselves in my absence. Mr. Yates speaks in dulcet tones but his legs are quite scrawny."

It was the fashion to talk so, in whips and circles; even though I had learned a more direct speech with Frances.

"Hey, you bill-and-cooers," called Geoffrey, who had come up stealthily behind us, and for a moment I did not know to which pair of us he was referring. "I've a bottle of wine deep in my rucksack. Care to join me?"

Do I relate this entire story when a guest of mine pulls from the stack this portrait of an old lover? Indeed I do not, for it is troubling to me still and I never make public that which I hold for private scrutiny.

Untitled

Frances gave me the plain maple box in which I keep these photos. I flattered myself at first: a country girl with so few possessions, such poor possessions, has chosen me to be the recipient of her most beloved dovetail! Of the homeliest order! I photographed her then and there in my bedroom, holding the gift out before her. As if the motion of giving could be so recorded. She looks surprised in this frame. Her pale, fledgling eyebrows are raised as if by the master puppeteer; she had no coquetry. Her eyes clouded—no, I could not fully read her face and I hid behind the camera for longer than was necessary. It was I who was ashamed when she said quite simply, "It was a box I never cared for."

II

1925

She had been promised a trip to Europe for the summer she was nineteen. But Malin arrived by train to Saskoba Falls and from there a ride to Garner in a motorcar with a sullen boy most likely her age but with a hay smell, she would write with dignified condescension, and a case of sunburn.

She forced her hand into her small black satchel to finger the letter in which had come the invitation: Will you join us in the wilds of New Hampshire? Broad fun, old-fashioned people. It's a virtue to be old-fashioned this summer. If you can't photograph the Tour Eiffel, there's sure to be a country pageant where the folk will never have seen a camera! Yours very truly, Roberto.

He was just Robert, really, but he would tease her to no end that she wouldn't see Rome this wheat-gold summer. He would never dare to mention her father's business, but he would talk endlessly of the ship he had sailed upon the summer before, when indeed her father might have purchased a small European country. But on no account would her father allow his daughter to accompany the jack-a-dandy, the attitudinarian Robert Yates to Europe.

She drew out the letter and scowled at her name in Robert's hand—like a cake with scalloped icing: he was almost a fop and why he came up here to summer—

well, it was a steep contrast to the city, she thought as she turned her head toward the country boy driving.

A sturdy cap cast a square shadow to his flat brow (he must be younger than she, after all); he was not used to being looked at and rushed to speak as he must have thought she wanted. "Apple orchards," he said as though it were one syllable, unknowing of its lacks or longings.

But he wasn't about to make some outburst. Nor was confession his vernacular. Malin sighed. Garner people would not be storytellers. "I'm Malin Nillsen," she said. "How do you do?"

"Asa Robinson."

"Well at least you've a name from our former century."

She was supposed to be in London. She was supposed to be in the French Alps. There were princes of places like Monaco, Torino, Milano. No towns in New Hampshire ended in "o." Robert and his gang—well, no secrets there. Asa Robinson in homemade pants, an unassuming farmhouse coming into view: built entirely for practicality. Nothing to recommend it to the heart or the eye, thought Malin.

"Is that it?" she said into the already tired suspense between them.

Asa Robinson pulled carefully off the road. A horse-drawn hay cart passed them. "Folks get choked with dust behind an automobile. Give them the right of way. For the one on foot you're to turn off the motor."

So Garner people would be walkers, thought Malin. Severe, as the boy next to her, but unhurried.

Well she knew why Robert had insisted she come. What her beau liked about her was she was game. She always tried the soup du jour; she once spent an after-noon playing canasta with his bedridden grandmother. He said he found her observations most amusing. More than once she had caught him using them as his own. ("Frances is like an Afghan hound," she would say rather adorably, the very first night, "who has left its lovely coat on the train, which has already left the station." And she would overhear Robert in the parlor,

("Typical: the country wench with the profile of an Afghan hound." The small crowd tittered and Malin changed her course. She would not join them in the parlor. Frances was still in the kitchen, pensive over the glistening silver plate. It was that mentation, self-counsel, had inspired Malin's characterization. But had Robert really overlooked her beauty? The high cheekbones and shapely mouth? Her hair was light and cold and fell to the small of her back even tied, as if to suffocate the braid, Malin thought, with an end of navy ribbon.)

But if he made her descriptions banal she had not yet noticed for she did love him. She felt a lovely rippling of anticipation—"The lover's bellyache," she had called it.

Mrs. Giddens was in the yard. There was no exchange of coins in public—the sum for the taxi service had been agreed on in the spring when the preparations were made to open the town for the summer season.

(There had been one Town Meeting in the middle of May, Malin would learn later, convened by the selectman whose particular charge was the problem of the summer people. He was Buck Herman, also storekeeper of Maude's

Penny Candy and Sportsman's Accessories, whose living was most gently accumulated—the native residents bought wool socks, hurricane lamps, and once or twice a year, replacement sinews for a snowshoe. Because he did not depend on summer people, who brought their own rifles and compasses, and because penny candy literally amounted to pennies, he could indeed afford to call them a problem.

(In attendance were those who took in boarders: Giddens, Whiting, Killam, Tobey, etc. and those who provided services such as hiking, swimming, fishing, and driver for hire, as young Asa Robinson, although the business was in decline.)

Mrs. Giddens hesitated before sketching a gesture of welcome. She blended in with the sallow yard around her. No, there was mint, that Malin knew, she could smell it, and a bald flagpole that made the yard tall if not handsome. There were no such women in the city. Ladies of New York were either beautiful because they were in the city or destitute because the city had made them so. Mrs. Giddens was at once impervious to her surroundings and made up of them. She was scooped out in the center and filled with the flour left on the board after forty years of kneading, baking.

It was suddenly dispiriting to imagine doling out the blather of first impressions to Roberto. It wasn't that she pitied Mrs. Giddens but that the woman withheld herself formidably. The body of a flour sack? Too easy, Malin reproached herself. Every country woman baked bread. No, Mrs. Giddens's innards were rich and ferric. They were twisted and wound around her heart just like Malin's.

"It's lovely here," said Malin.

Mrs. Giddens addressed Asa. "She's arrived on Good Roads Day."

"My father says he's not seen such damage from the frost heaves for a decade," said Asa.

Robert and company would have already done their close reading of Asa, Huck Finned him, Hester Prynned him, as they said in the city. But Mrs. Giddens was hers. They would have given Mrs. Giddens no notice.

The country woman drew a sprig of mint from the bodice of her apron and this gesture collided awkwardly with Asa's lurch forward to land the city valise at the hostess's feet. Malin felt strangely that she should rush to Mrs. Gidden's defense. "Oh do bring the luggage inside," she scolded Asa.

Inside the farmhouse was dank and cold. The doorways were low and Mrs. Giddens bent her head reflexively to pass beneath them. They ended in the summer kitchen, suddenly bright and busy with a tall girl supervising two young children in the hulling of mounded quarts of strawberries.

"Frances will show you to your room," said Mrs. Giddens, already receding. The tall girl took her place without acknowledging the order.

"Are the others about?" Malin said. The stairs were ramrod straight—no gentle spiral. They were high enough to bring your knees up in an ungainly prancing manner; shallow so you were forced to place your feet sideways. Each with a tread nailed to the old wood, a creak as if from a corseted pilgrim.

Malin would share a room with another girl in Robert's gang—a cousin, she thought, or a cousin's cousin—ha!—she thought to share the joke with Mrs. Giddens's solemn daughter—

("Solemn!" cried Robert. "Sullen's the kindest to us she's been yet this summer. Malin, I predict your generosity shall spoil the natives.")

"They'll convene here for supper," said Frances. Then she left the bedroom without warning. Malin heard her light step stop halfway down the passage and a shoe squeaked slightly on the well-waxed floor. "You won't be needing lip rouge or other trappings for our suppers. We're simple here." Frances's voice was soft and yet each word distinct; the command was not lost on Malin.

Malin looked about the room under the eaves. Roberto's cousin's things were spread upon a low double bureau—a costly abalone hand mirror, hat ribbon, bottle of eau de toilette, and several containers of lip rouge. Malin picked one up to check the color: burnished cherry. There was a long, speckled mirror on the wall, tarnished and dizzyingly distorted. Malin's hearty build became voluptuous in the reflection, her clear skin taut over a harmonious oval visage lost in the pockmarks of the mirror. Her eyes, she knew, were of unusual brightness, set wide, and her blondness was even astounding. She found herself frowning to imitate Frances's solemnity, found her rosiness in the glass suddenly vulgar, her lushness of figure uncourtly. Well she would wear burnished cherry to supper to spite the flat-chested girl who called out a dress code.

Geoffrey Ross was in competition with Robert Yates to be the life of the party. They were each more boisterous than the other but Malin found herself distracted by the quietest member of this strange summer household. At supper, Frances was a doll cut from newsprint and painted impressionistically. She flattened herself against the murky walls and only moved when the boarders were at the height of a joke or a parry.

Geoffrey had a way with women in the city, Malin knew, a reputation that he was eager to live up to. "Frances Giddens," he nudged Malin when Frances was in the kitchen fetching more bread or potatoes. "So far our favorite scarecrow."

"Miss Giddens to you, Mr. Ross," quipped Angelina Maddox.

"Miss Giddens!" he called. "Tell me the truth. Does anyone at this table make you giddy?"

"A stupid play, old Geoffy," said Robert. "Dear Miss Giddens," he adopted a false fatherly tone. "Do tell us about your town's habit of Good Roads Day." All heads turned toward the pale paper doll caught listing reluctantly in the doorway.

"Ah-ha," said Geoffrey Ross. "The notice from the town clerk lies on the kitchen table. Citizens gather thy shovels. Apple pie and brown bread after you've put your back into it. Boys, to the drainage ditches!" Geoffrey's color was high from flask wine and bragging.

It was more than Robert Yates could stand. Malin watched his mouth twitching. He rose with stilted dignity. Geoffrey quit his oration as Robert approached the girl Frances. He bent his knee before her and took her hand.

"Tsk, tsk," said Carl Adler, one of the others.

"My lovely Miss Giddens," Robert said in a stage whisper. "We city folk can be as promiscuous as poison ivy. Please forgive my gentleman friend. If you'd care to give us a more gentle rendition of your Good Roads Day—well, you'll join us in the parlor after this fine meal?"

Malin saw that Frances was trembling.

Robert was looking only at the slender hand as if it were a carved fetish.

Malin had never trembled with her hand inside a man's hand. Most likely she had never even held Robert's hand. By the elbow was the fashionable manner. She thought his hand must be hot and dry, he used talcum powder.

Carl Adler's girl, Katrina Howlander, was trying to catch her eye: a jealous outburst would make fine entertainment.

Much later in the evening Malin sneaked outside to take a smoke. The darkness was complete. As a child she had given the stars much thought. She had a lacquered letter box and on the inside of the lid the night sky was painted with glitter against a dense blue background. Lately the consideration of these universal mysteries seemed trite and her imagination was reserved for the right she felt she had to human love.

It wasn't that Robert Yates thought a woman shouldn't smoke but rather that she shouldn't want to.

She had looked back directly at Katrina Howlander. "Oh come, Katrina. You enjoy the sport too." But Frances, for whom the barb was carefully sharpened, appeared not to have heard, so transfixed was she by her hand in a man's hand. She had long eyes of such a dark blue or gray that it was impossible to tell if they were portals to that same night sky or if they were, beyond Malin's prying watch, looking inward.

⧉•⧉

In a moment her lovely Roberto would emerge from the glowing harbor with his arms outstretched like a child playing blindman's bluff. This is how it happened at home in her father's tiny garden. She would stub out the cigarette when his body blocked the light from the door.

But no, it was Miss Howlander picking her way down the granite stoop. Malin leaned back into the hedge of lilac and ferns. Katrina caught the slight rustle and earthy tobacco smell. "Malin. May I have your confidence?" She wore a strident scent of lily of the valley.

Malin shrugged.

Katrina was too distracted to note Malin's evasion. "You and Robert are nearly engaged, aren't you? It's a little girl's concern, but perhaps you'll advise me."

(Robert had not touched her in that way since she arrived. He wasn't a man who had it as a need, he had explained, but sought it as a complex pleasure. After the first time she had fled the downtown hotel before he could minister to her, provide requisite and gallant apology. She had not been ashamed to dress in the room, in front of him, and this had shocked him deeply. She walked fast and blind, her legs cold, her stomach hot and roiling.

She had thought: to wash it off I must jump in the Hudson River. There is nothing else for it. And an instant later she knew such a thought was the last girlish thought she would manufacture. She turned herself deliberately back toward the hotel. Robert was fully dressed, asleep upon the reddened bedsheets.)

"I fear the boys will do something they'll regret once we return home," Katrina's whine reached her. "They've quite lost their comportment. They've fashioned a lodgings, framed of pine boughs, piled inside with dry leaves, a most rank and oily smelling sheepskin filched from Mrs. Giddens." She took a breath but did not continue. It was as if she were disappointed with her own rendition, not its veracity but its lack of magic. She had told it to the letter—Malin could see she was sure, but there was no way to put into words: was it her own mantle, cape, light coat that he would spread out for her?

"Boys will make such traps," Malin said matter-of-factly. "Who knows what they get—stray dogs and tomcats." Her eyes had been accustomed to the dark for quite some time. She stole a look—Katrina bore her silky features with measured patience. "Well of course, there must be a lure." Malin said lightly. "A flask of brandy?"

Suddenly she had no desire to give advice or to hear a confession. It seemed wrong here. As if in a church, or near a sleeping baby. She rose and shook her little shawl and gave Katrina a touch on the arm as if to dismiss her.

The party had moved to the parlor. Robert stood up when he saw her. "Miss Nillsen and Miss Howlander.

You've just missed our evening's program on Good Roads but here's the brilliant part. It happens again tomorrow."

The flask of brandy had been going round. Robert rarely offered but never let it pass by him untasted. If he said the things he thought aloud he would be considered arrogant. By keeping certain comparisons to himself (but he had shared them with Malin. Their echoes seemed to her now outrageous. "Are we the only ones, my Dear, who make love in broad daylight?") he managed a humble demeanor that was de rigueur to a man of his standing. (It had been only once in the day and with great mortification. It had never been in the out-of-doors. He would say that was for children.)

III

Malin dreamed of apple orchards gone up in powdery clouds of blossom—the drive with Asa Robinson a gentle motoring through artfully curvaceous meadows, the solemn girl Frances as an old-world peasant goddess. When she woke up the bed was even narrower than it had been the night before. Not a bed for stoking dreams, lingering.

The city girls, all three of them nearly or newly twenty, would follow a path through the woods across the Abbott Farm and intercept the Good Roads crew at a bridge one of the toiling Giddens sons had suggested.

(Bridges froze first. The dirt packed hard as stone blistered with frost heaves like armored molehills. The bridge was in no danger, Mr. Giddens said, it was the automobile could be pitched into this fierce tributary of the Saskoba.)

Malin thought they were quite too pleased with themselves but she too looked forward to the natural entertainment. By midmorning the girls set off, Katrina designated to carry a simple lunch in burlap.

Malin was effortlessly ahead a half hour into the hike. At first the forest seemed to her artificially dark, like a theater, perennial evening. One dreamed in this light.

So, one dreamed in the out-of-doors here, not between the bedsheets.

Or, it was luminous as a cathedral. The trees were stained glass windows, filtering a muted, dappled green.

How different trees were of different religions, she fancied. (Robert would find such reporting dull, but she went on anyway.)

The beech serene, silky, and virginal as Katrina Howlander. The forest floor reflected light like sand: bright and dry and easy walking. The fallen leaves, ivory and tan, were like the wood shavings of an old icon carver.

A pine grove was shades dimmer, blue even in the morning. What sort of pines were these? Feathery and wet, almost buoyant, a delightful, kerchiefed congregation. The trunks oozed thick resin and the ground was busy with ants, small sticky pinecones.

When she gathered a pace she kept at it and in that way found herself far ahead, wrapped in private reverie. Perhaps she would not have caught herself dreaming if she hadn't been startled out of it by an unmistakably human scuffle. (Dreaming of someone, not Roberto, for Roberto would never lead her blind down the banks of a stream past midnight to lie in leaves and old sheepskin, but it certainly wasn't Carl Adler she wanted, was it anyone then—she stopped short and it was then she heard the deliberate rustle.)

"They don't come all at once," a voice warbled out. "They stay together and don't care for young ladies. They never take their shirts off."

"Miss Giddens," Malin called. "Wherever are you?"

"Oh here and there." A pause and silence. "You may as well turn back you know. Or a warmed stone wall is good for sitting." She came into view. Slight and fresh in the forest, not the drudge she looked working for her mother. "Have you heard a blue jay screech for pleasure?" Her look mischievous.

"I'd never thought why they call," Malin said almost humbly.

"Oh they're like the young ladies directly behind you. No men in Garner will mind them."

They reached the bridge and rested, leaning upon its iron railing. They shared their lunch with Frances. Angelina Maddox let her hair down for all women are Artemis in the forest, she said. They waited for an hour and Frances would say nothing.

Finally they heard an engine's throaty braying and then the automobile rumbled into view. The young ladies brightened although their hands in the shade and after the lunch were almost chilly. Malin looked around and Frances had vanished. (There were three men across the bench seat of a doleful and sputtering automobile that coasted to a stop at the edge of the bridge. The driver strode the length of the bridge to address them. "We've the repair of this bridge that concerns us." The other two remained in the automobile, long necks in a fixed position.

(Katrina squeezed her hand. "Pardon us," Malin said. She thought she heard Frances's rare laugh from somewhere deeper in the forest, stifled by dense brush, dark branches.)

There was an invitation to attend the square dance on Saturday. They all thought what a joke and agreed on the spot to wear their traveling clothes, as these were the finest they'd brought to Garner.

Malin had seen the Town Hall where the dance would take place and had thought it was the church. Sparse in architecture; no tree or flowering shrub softened it or alleviated the sense one had of an amateur line drawing, unidimensional.

"Old Giddens would like a word with us," Geoffrey Ross whispered all around. Angelina, petite and lustrous, said to Malin that Mr. Giddens held the key to her heart.

"My country heart," she winked.

City people and country people lived in different eras, but Mr. Giddens might be a time traveler, at ease as he was with the boarders. He entertained them with evening recitals on the organ even though he knew none of the popular songs from last season or the season before. He played "Tenting Tonight" and "Auld Lang Syne" as if they were composed expressly for contemporary lovers. His dignity did not allow him to notice Angelina's manner and it was, of course, for this reason that she continued her flirtations. And yet Malin had seen him with Robert and Geoffrey—three tall men through a hay field; rolling gaits and half smiles.

There were handshakes for the men as he entered the parlor and Angelina spoke up: "What a wonderful scent arises from freshly mown hay!" So she wanted to be considered dreamy, thought Malin.

"A scent from the hay. Of course," he echoed.

"You wanted a word with us about the square dance," said Geoffrey, eager to add to his stock of country lore.

"A word about the dance." Then it was his style to always make an echo.

He is a mourner, Malin thought. She recognized her own father, the weathering of persistent sadness. But if

Geoffrey Ross could be cruel he was also right to call Mr. Giddens a clown—he seemed to mock the very crowd he performed for.

"Forgive me if my words are suited for another coterie," Mr. Giddens began. "No drunkenness, no rowdiness of that particular order. The fellowship of Giddens boarders shall comport themselves with decency." His eyes twinkled.

"You flatter us," cried Angelina. "We're such a stultified bunch. We shan't make a ripple."

Malin saw that Frances had entered the room quietly. It was plain even on her careful face she thought Angelina a hussy or a fool. "Frances," Malin spoke across the room. "Will you be joining us?"

"I'll bet your daughter is a real high-stepper," said Angelina for general appeal.

"You are permitted to speak directly to her," said Mr. Giddens.

Geoffrey bridled. "If the ladies would excuse us while we do business."

"Shall the girls have dance cards then?" said Angelina. "Is there a line for me already? I'm a sensation with the Virginia Reel."

Was it as simple as the fact that Mr. Giddens was unflappable? thought Malin. "The Virginia Reel is for Virginians," he said. "There is the business of admission. Buck Herman, enduring selectman, shall be at the door."

"A charge for admission!" yodeled Robert Yates with mock indignation.

"Without fail."

"But we're official summer citizens," Geoffrey joined.

So there would be a lark. The summer crowd from Giddens's would give these provident New Englanders a taste of their own medicine. Malin was amazed to see how fast and how gleefully Geoffrey arranged it. It involved all the usual ruses: alluring ladies, ladies taken ill, a cry of fire. "It's pennies to you, Roberto," Malin said.

He pulled her in and squeezed her sportily. "It's principles, my Swedish princess."

They called Asa Robinson their chauffeur in high humor. "Oh, we have been bored silly, haven't we," said Angelina in relief as they eased down Hunter's Hill to the Town Hall on Main Street.

Angelina walked the path from street to entrance alone but for an outlandish parasol. Malin had wanted no part in the prank but in the end she could not resist donating her recent Chinatown acquisition. It had fuming dragons chasing each other's tails with almost sexual vigor, Robert commented. Angelina placed her feet one in front of the other as if she were a tightrope walker and when she finally reached the gatekeeper her color was high and the sun was setting.

(Buck Herman was the gatekeeper. Malin, the only child of a man of all businesses, recognized that Buck Herman's store on Main Street served something yet more essential to the town than what was sold there.

(This was not a town that welcomed impresarios or orphans. The sobriety of history or the reticence of a starched white farmhouse with a taut and frugal smile afforded a peace in the lives of folk who did not put peace into words but sat on front porches and supported local businesses, not for moral reasons, but to save gasoline or the horse's iron shoe. Asa Robinson had pointed out Buck Herman's farmhouse over the banter of the boarders. Narrow shoulders, slate roofing, granite blocks in the foundation. Asa said, "Only uses a cord of wood a winter," but Malin imagined that it creaked contentedly for it was built in a time when winters were colder and evenings were longer than in this loose Century.

(To be a good gatekeeper one had to go away and then come back. By the end of her stay Malin would divine that Herman had made such a journey but of where he'd been or what he'd done no one ever asked. When he returned he savored a landscape that had made sense in 1729, Main Street a bold gesture when gesture was a force stronger than the materials used to illustrate it.

(Perhaps, Malin thought, he saw Main Street like the mast on the boat a child sets upon his father's pond—the town of Garner was shaped like a sail filled with small winds. He published a pamphlet for his selectman's race the year he returned and it was still displayed on a table in the entryway of the Giddens farmhouse along with several editions of a surveyor's map and the library's summer hours. Malin had watched Frances dusting and rearranging the exhibition.)

Malin, eschewing a part, stayed in the automobile with Asa Robinson after the others dispersed behind various trees, a milk truck with Saskoba lettering. Robert had said, why, she was all mournsome, dog in the manger. Had she adopted the gravity of Garner? The tragic anhedonia?

The others wanted to use their city prowess to show the town that its dense weave could be balled in a fist or gathered and draped into an irreverent costume. They sought an opening in the stone wall not knocked by a horse or disassembled purposely but because of a job carelessly executed. But Malin wanted it intact.

She could hear Angelina's merriment. "Mr. Herman! My beau's inside. Will you fetch him?"

Well that was the easy strike, thought Malin. Or rather, like going right to ball four. Angelina's pitch was indeed that perfect. Malin slipped out of the automoblile and up the worn path behind her in time to see Buck Herman, in a suit both tailored and mindfully pressed in the annals of the last century, recede into the dark swallow of the Town Hall.

Carl Adler emerged from his mock hiding spot with a tap step and pinched Malin's waist lightly. "All my money in my pocket," he said.

She let him go inside without her. The others followed shortly. After a time Buck Herman resumed his post. He propped the door open with the piano bench, polished ebony with use. Fiddle music strayed out into the warm night, and scattered clapping. Moths spiraled toward the lighted hall and Malin imagined she was back in time and such a soiree held all the possibility for her future. She shuddered to think of Robert Yates (the others had their girls) with his arm around another flame, small and straight.

She eased herself down upon the cool granite steps just apart from Buck Herman. She felt tired from such antics, not the suspense but that the high jinks were misplaced here. She imagined the sweaty brows of the dancers not unlike the perspiration that beaded and fell, beaded and fell, when they were working. She was still enough now for the breeze to find her. How could anyone stomp his feet and swing his girl after a day of ceaseless, almost penitent, laboring?

↦ IV ↤

Without pause for consideration, Malin began to emulate Frances's dress and carriage. She had lent a lovely charcoal silk jacket with a modern riding cut to Katrina and then found she didn't want it back. She became wholly absorbed in studying the blockish angle of Frances's wool cape across her shoulders. Black wool in summer? And then suddenly she was cold; or she wished to feel the intimate warmth of her own body. Frances, self-contained as a pond turtle. Or you could lay the cape down and have a bed.

Asa was a somber chaperone but now she felt she could get more out of him in his native silence than with all her practiced and stylish questioning. He drove her to Buck Herman's store where she purchased not only the cape but the high, lead-soled and lead-buttoned shoes that, by their contrast, made Frances's calves thin as drinking straws.

Malin knew she would be expected to announce her engagement in the coming season but she noticed how she and Robert seemed to drift apart here in New Hampshire. Robert and Carl could play cards through a morning; Malin occupied herself with a book or a small task eked out of the dour Mrs. Giddens.

"Such a pile of carrots, Mrs. Giddens. Really, I've nothing else to do. I could snip their tails off in a flash."

"Certainly not, Miss Nillsen. Frances and I must make a living."

To admit that they too were creatures dependent on money—even just for food, shelter—was garrulous for this hostess.

"But I must learn to cook, Mrs. Giddens! What am I to do when I marry?"

It wasn't true, Malin already cooked for her father on occasion and had a natural intuition for tastes and smells. But there the quiet Frances might take the bait.

"You've no skills at all in the kitchen?"

"Before I came to Garner I didn't know that an egg came in a shell." It was a bald lie and she warmed to it.

"Do you mean to say that you found an eggshell in your breakfast?" Now she had drawn Frances to the middle of the summer kitchen. Malin caught her eye. The urge to smile was like a balloon in her stomach, but instead she took one step inside the doorway.

Mrs. Giddens wheeled about. "The summer kitchen's for the staff, Miss Nillsen." There was neither humor nor warning in her voice. Just this: things stay as they are.

Now I've lost the marriage thread, thought Malin. So she'd simply pull a new one from the weave. "Mrs. Giddens," she said directly. "Have you observed how Mr. Yates fancies your daughter?"

Then the breezy kitchen fell away and the two women in aprons of some remnant of rough material left the room by floating upward, impossibly, through the slate roof, and when Malin rushed outside to catch them there was only a solitary Giddens son chopping wood in the yard; an axe that beat time with metronomic precision.

That night Frances did not serve dinner but it was she who approached Malin the next morning and said gravely,

"You may help with the lunch if you'll not tease me."

Malin had rescued and nurtured stray cats and dogs in her childhood in the city but befriending Frances, she admitted, was surprisingly dissimilar. Frances wanted nothing from Malin—the dish of milk set down on the floor went unsniffed, unheeded. She cared not for petty affection, but could be enticed to lengths of conversation neither quite dialogues nor expressly monologues either. Malin would try to incite her passions: Don't you long to see the city? Who will you marry here? Asa Robinson? Don't mind the slick Mr. Yates. The imbecile Mr. Adler.

Frances had a lovely chuckle like scarce water through pebbles.

"I'd go to England to see if my ancestors possess this nose," Frances said. She touched hers, small and straight, the nose of an unerring Pilgrim. "But I'm waiting for a certain letter."

"A beau, then? Tell me!"

"From a mentor of the spirit, a writer."

"Would you not even consider Mr. Yates if he asked you?"

Malin didn't know what drove her toward pawning off Roberto. She turned it over in her mind before sleep: was she testing Robert against another woman, albeit a girl and a strange one, to see from another angle his mettle? He had never shown interest in their young hostess. She noticed that he sometimes tipped her father exorbitantly and the change rattled in Frances's outstretched dish. But if Robert requested a melody and the doleful Mr. Giddens did not know how to play it and was forced to resort to a Civil War marching song through which to purge his embarrassment, Robert said he felt the old man had tried sportingly and was to be rewarded for such effort.

Frances lowered her eyes when she moved about the dining table or through the candlelit parlor. Her lashes threw shadows of wavering flora down her pointed face but Malin imagined she saw the girl's chest rise and be held when she paused briefly before Robert.

After a week of balancing precariously on the threshold of the summer kitchen, Malin was allowed to sit at the long trestle table and work her way through a bowl of mercilessly scrubbed potatoes for the soup that was an inevitable precursor to the noontime meal. As she had hoped, Mrs. Giddens began to think of her as a friend for her daughter and when it was discovered that there were only two years between them, the woman confessed, uncharacteristically, that there had been another daughter who shared the year of Malin's birth but who had passed early in that first wet winter. Malin knew that it was not for her that this information had been gently tipped out but for Frances. A mother was saying not so much that life is harder than it looks to a summer boarder, for instance, but that life's hardships can be borne for years on end before incidental, casual, confession.

Route Seven would deliver you to Maynard. Rural folk had no waste that could not be repaired or composted, but there was a pit in a field too wet to hay off Route Seven that would receive, after the Great War, the final, hopeless bones of a nineteenth-century plow, or a broken trunk abandoned by a summer lodger that could not, for one reason or another, be used as a planter for February seedlings or cold storage for cabbages or as an infant's cradle. Frances told Malin on the way there with two rusted washboards and a spool of molded baler twine in the cart that her father had been one of the ones to dig it two years prior on Good Roads Day.

"Or 'Days,' as your Mr. Yates would have it," Frances added.

The depth was determined between the selectmen of Garner and Maynard, Buck Herman leading the vote for a shallower pit so that it would not endanger the horses of men who wished to retrieve something. "For one man's waste is another man's treasure," and it surprised and pleased Malin to no end that Frances attempted to imitate Buck Herman's singularly hollow timbre.

As they approached Maynard, Malin noted meaner, meatier dogs roped to trees in dirt yards and more old farmhouses gone to silver. She felt vaguely cheated by the discrepancy. She had been compiling carefully a photographic record and now here was a broader view of New Hampshire. She hadn't thought to bring the camera and all its apparatus but she watched greedily as Route Seven lent itself for a lackluster stretch that called itself Main Street. The middle of Frances's brothers, James, who was driving the horse, called back that the pit was just the other side of town: from this and the way that Frances's eyes darted about Malin understood that the better men had got to Garner.

They passed a filling station where houndish men idled. "Indeed," said Frances in a low voice, "our planning Ordinances specify that there shall be no petroleum-based commerce in Garner."

"You learn such things in a one-room schoolhouse," James called to Malin, laughing.

"But the train stops here," Malin called back. "Why didn't I see Maynard on my New York schedule?"

"Only freight; from the west, Pennsylvania."

True, it would not be a place that welcomed travelers. There was no sign, only a simple tin-roofed shelter you could pull a truck under to load or unload quickly, make way for the next man.

"But a tramp or a salesman could jump a freighter," said Frances.

A derailed train car housed a lunchroom. Malin saw a heavy woman in the doorway as they passed. Just the contour of her breast, she thought, betrayed that she was not from Garner. Such a woman would have to put up her feet for swollen ankles. From such a woman would emanate a musky well-being: sleep would not be illicit, would figure into her day. Yes, Frances's eyes were trained upon her.

"LaFrenier," she said, the way a man would say it. "Canadian."

James Giddens whipped up the horse. "Canada's a long mile from New Hampshire."

"She hunts deer with a pitchfork," said Frances.

James laughed. "It used to be a great sport to frighten our sister."

"They have no guns in Canada because they are pacifists. She fleeced us of our steel-made hayfork," Frances said, rustling with humor.

"There's not so much work here for them with the mills closing. Still they trickle down," said James. "Accidentally."

Malin had expected a huge gash in the forest, an empty reservoir, from the way that Frances had warned her of the pit. But the people of Tewksboro County generated almost no waste. At the end of a narrow dirt track there was an indentation the size of a modest farmhouse in a marshy, overgrown field of ten acres. James got down and unloaded their unwanted items, poked about for salvage, came up with a shovel cracked from head to handle. Malin thought he hefted it like an old friend, and she and Frances made room for it in the cart. They watched a pair of mangy, gull-like birds circle the clearing.

"It's no place to take a guest," said James.

"She'll make her own mind," Frances replied in a distinctly plain fashion.

Robert Yates was a redhead and as such had a symbolic temper that Malin had never seen lost but she had seen him use it to his advantage. When Malin suggested that he employ it oftener and on her behalf Robert told her he had a hole in his heart any doctor could hear by placing a trained ear on his chest and for this reason he would never be a passionate lover.

"But I can be true," he said, and Malin, being three years younger than she was this summer, felt she could not risk asking if he spoke in jest.

And yet while he maintained, "I am not the fighting type," he had great virility by which Malin had been "swept away" when they consummated—if not the very first time then after that on more than one occasion.

"Swept away?" Robert said, pushing up onto one elbow. He had rented them another proper room in a proper if middling hotel. The curtains were flimsy and blowing even though the one small window remained swollen shut on the first dry day of spring. "Swept away. Is my love a wind, Malin?" and he gestured theatrically toward the thin curtains, "or a river, and I some hapless island."

"So poetic, Roberto. Promise to take me to Europe—I shall have more practice there and be able to tell you precisely." Her voice was warm and so he put a hand on her forehead and bowed his head in an awkward aching motion that for her had nearly broken the spell of their lovemaking.

Then they would separate. Laughing, they stood outside the hotel with their backs touching in a kind of reverse embrace and went off one north and one south along the busy, clamorous avenue.

But this summering in Garner was perhaps to have been different. They both knew there would be no city to fracture their attention for one another—at home, they would go weeks without seeing each other, relying on an

Having caught Malin off her usual guard he continued jauntily in order to regale the whole table. "Young Asa Robinson runs a fine taxi service to the surrounding towns and at a reasonable rate. The dumpyard at Maynard provides quixotic entertainment. The spiritual or whimsical search of a people is always recorded in what they discard. Has anyone noticed how little is gone to waste from this very table?"

"You are mean-spirited and insinuating, Robert," said Malin.

"You describe yourself, Miss Nillsen. The manner in which you left our Frances to find her way home through the primordial forest."

Carl Adler was fond of adopting a benevolent fatherly aspect when called upon to console a woman. It was not original but rather the fashion among the urban elite and Malin had encountered it before and considered it both affected and passé. "May I?" he bowed at the doorway of her room and Malin thought what a coincidence she had seen a wild turkey for the first time just yesterday, a bird too big for its britches in a literal, ungainly manner.

("There, Miss Nillsen," Frances had whispered. "If you were a hunter I'd say you'd flushed it, and fine work. You see it doesn't know what it was startled by. But its thicket has been parted and it feels as though it's walking through a universe. It's alarmed; but do you suppose it's truly frightened?"

("I prefer the eagle for our country's emblem," Malin had said, not caring, suddenly, to speak of fear.)

"You're not to lose your young man, my dear. He's only been brusque because he fears to lose you. I spoke to him about singling you out in front of all of us, but he does consider the six of us quite intimate," said Adler.

"You think I've taken offense?"

"There is some stir among us regarding your absences from our daily routines and our outings."

"Some stir?" Malin couldn't help laughing.

"Please refrain from hysterics. It's not for such that I'm training to be a doctor." He allowed himself an avuncular ahem.

"Have you come to arrange a marriage between Mr. Yates and me?" Now Malin's light-blue eyes were restored of their spark.

"I should have thought something like that was very nearly arranged."

"Prior to your intrusion?" Now he would take offense and she would have led him off the track and directly down the incline or into the bushes or the ditch or the swamp or whatever hard-to-extract-oneself place she intended to leave him, the turkey. He was old and blindered before he'd ever been young.

Across the yard to the barn she caught up with Frances who was swinging two pails. Her arms were bare; thin and white and still muscled like a girl's arms from climbing trees and doing her mother's errands. Malin's own arms had long since gathered weight and a shapeliness that would cause Robert to squeeze them in public if he were that sort of man.

"Frances!" she called as she approached. "You'll come back with me to New York, won't you?"

The girl had a spring in her step and her pointed chin seemed to Malin to teeter upon her neck in an exquisitely sculptural manner. "Will you?" Malin repeated. "I shall arrange the loveliest of parties where a dozen gentlemen will put their lips to your knuckles—" she couldn't even pretend for Frances's sake that she believed in such romance, but it was imperative that Frances come. A girl who could summon a man to the edge of a clearing. Could set a man afire. In her quietude could spin a forest around herself and speak with the sudden verity of a summer thunder.

Frances slowed until Malin was a half-step behind her. Gave a laugh like a baby's silver rattle.

"That thunderstorm has put you in a fine form, Miss Nillsen." She lifted her pale brows so that her forehead became a rippled beach and Malin could read nothing upon it but ripples.

Part Three
New Residents

I

At the turn of each season Willard Heald went over the records to see that Buck Herman had entered the applicants. Each year, the Ordinances allowed one new name to the census. Willard's perusal would be on a day when the proprietor of Maude's Penny Candy and Sportsman's Accessories was out to some farm looking the trees over: he'd had his training at the University of New Hampshire.

(What was a gall and what were carpenter ants and what a rare disease that called for the pruning of specific branches. Herman would certainly pay a visit to the new residents. He would go in the season of the soft pulpy caterpillars that fell from the outermost branches of some maple. Rain would make an epilogue to his visit. He would go again after the first snow and finally in the silent lungs of winter.)

The two men stood over the glass counter where a cornucopia of penny candy was flanked by hunting rifles and buck knives and waders and decoys. "A warm spell surely fouls the springtime," said Herman.

"Good for business but bad for the spring," he went on, musingly. "Like a schoolgirl dressed up to be a woman."

The whole earth caved in that March. There was melting that went five feet under. Herman had crossed Main Street in waders off his own shelf.

"The weather will express herself in water," said Heald.

A cup of coffee was passed from one man to the other. Maude the spaniel awoke from a hunting dream and let out a bark still half in a weasel field and to chide her master for having company. On another day, thought Heald, Buck Herman would declare that this man and dog was the original combination. A pairing that happened long before Eve came, rib first, into the garden. But today, Heald could sense without asking that Herman was going to Abigail's.

The Lilacs of Abigail Joslin
(*Our Townspeople, by Willard Heald*)

What grows freely:
Squash, apple
Black-eyed Susan

Common issue:
Clover,
Vetch, and milkweed

A good woman
Turns any weed
To the use of her household

But Abigail Joslin
Imported
Lilac

"Read out your verse, Willard," said Buck Herman.
"It's only a scribble," the postman muttered disgustedly.

And yet, the lithe-bodied fragrance that filled his head with grayish purple. An open dormer window, sound of bees heavy with pollen, newly washed bed linen.

When he first discovered a girl, as a young man, and not even into his whiskers, her lips for tender discourse, her scent was always lilac.

Heald locked the door parsimoniously when Herman left, and afternoon silence fell quickly.

The dusky upstairs office smelled of cheap chocolate, coffee, leather, rag wool, wood floors soaked and dried through how many winters. Herman's desk was worn with use like a personal item of clothing. The postman settled before it with a pile of cryptic files and the distant view of the paper mill down the Saskoba River.

(There was talk it would be closing. He could count the Garner employees on one hand and they were the transient folk of French Canadian descent—a few bundled figures crossing and recrossing Main Street on their lunch hour—no faces and no voices.

(It was not local men who ran it. The windows of the great brick edifice had always seemed to Heald extravagant; too much glass never bodes well for a business. He imagined how the windows would dissolve into the sand of their origin.)

He picked up the hourglass on Buck Herman's desk. There had been no new residents in Garner for several years. Well, as he had said before, he was a man of the boundaries. He might have reminded anyone who challenged him what had happened to Abigail Joslin, Franklin

Abbott. Such fateful letters of introduction were thread-bare from his own fretful rereading.

Abby Joslin had loved a wiry, dark-haired man named Passarro. Heald remembered working a haying with him long ago—the way the men stared when he stripped off his shirt and revealed back and chest as thick with hair as an animal. He guzzled water like an animal too, and turned his face up to the sun at midday while the other men worked bowed, beneath shadow-casting hat brims.

He had proposed to clear-cut every last one of the Joslin acres. At Town Meeting every man would have voiced the same reaction: But the saplings? The big trees could fetch a fair price, and a sense of commerce in an outsider might eventually be forgiven. But the saplings? To lay waste an entire generation? "Despite what you city folk may think of us," had said Buck Herman, a sapling himself but already with wire-rimmed spectacles, "we are keener on the future than any hot-bellied industrial-ist. Our children do not flee to the cities."

It was later they found out Passarro was not from any city and then Willard Heald vowed to close the gates indiscriminately. There was no use sorting outsiders. None of them knew the value of the sapling.

It was not even the lumber Passarro wanted. He had proposed to build a replication of a Red Indian lodge upon the Joslin mountain. "But we have no Red Indians," said the elder Buck Herman judiciously—as if there was the possibility to resurrect them.

Passarro's voice was vinegar: "A gambling house." He would have been met with potent silence had it not been for the pitiful smile of old man Joslin, Abby's father, who longed to please his only daughter.

"Come to your senses, brothers!" cried Passarro. Every man looked askance, avoided each other's eyes at this repelling intimation. They were not brothers.

City folk would trade their dollars at the door for wooden checkers, Heald recalled. With these they would make their bets against the house and it was with these they would be paid their winnings.

"Upon their departure," crowed Passarro, "we'll decide how many checkers buys a greenback dollar!"

"Garner folk may be skinflints but they are not crooks," said the elder Buck Herman. His wry smile was a rarity for one of his stock. The postman remembered the way the young men hung on his words—he had mastered the art of public self-deprecation while he built himself up from the inside.

Passarro was the foul dandruff from a smoke-emitting mushroom, said Heald, and the elder Herman had allowed a smile. The outsider gone in the night without Abby once the Joslin land was denied him.

II

Between Giddens and Heald was Abbott for
whom the road had been named when there
were still vast expanses of land across the
entire country lost in separate unnamed
midnights.

Abbott's land was poorer than either of his
two neighbors'.

—*A postman's ruminations*

(He never interrupted his mail route to write his
thoughts—the writing was strictly for indoors and
evening. A white hand bared in such a way seemed to the
postman vulnerable, almost prurient, like the possum
with its hairless nose and tail. But he fancied his thoughts
arrived ready for transcription so that he could no longer
distinguish between what was haloed in ink and what
murmured like smoke in the imagination.)

But while I, Willard Heald, had long since given up
anything but a kitchen plot and Giddens more recently
but almost as thoroughly dismissed agricultural pursuits
or livestock, Abbott had kept his handful of sheep, clus-
ter of blood-stained chickens, and the single horse that
survived the fire. He was more of a pony, with thick
bangs and a slow waltz.

(There was no dog; Abbott had not enough words for a dog, thought Willard.)

Of the three farmsteads only Giddens had success with children: Abbott's ponderous son had come of age and gone looking for his mother; Mrs. Heald was tight-lipped on that subject but Heald suspected their child-lessness was of her intention.

There were rare times Heald had occasion to join in the talk of men who were never idle—it was noted among them that the particular constellation of Abbott Road would die with the next generation. And how long could a farm be a farm without its vegetables and its animals and its hardworking children?

The barn still stood on Abbott's place but the house he had given up to the fire that had consumed all domestic traces of the homestead.

It was ten years that could have been twenty since the departure of Margaret White Abbott. A lean-to had gradually accumulated against the back of the barn and when Buck Herman and the neighbor Giddens saw that it was no longer being added to they took it as a sign that the man was ready to be visited by his neighbors. It was the week preceding Good Roads Day, when the first cut had been dried and tedded and dried and baled and hauled up to the eaves of swallow-filled haylofts, that the men arrived on the place with lumber from the Tuttle sawmill.

"There are tragedies from which a man becomes too old to recover," said Abbott, protesting. He had a narrow forehead like a priest. His hair was long and gray and his eyes bright as if with fever.

"Tragedy has nothing to do with a roof over the flour that makes your bread," said Tuttle, hard worker and practical wordsmith.

Heald thought now how they might have come up sooner, at least trailed him home once from Maude's Penny Candy and Sportsman's Accessories, but these were men who did nothing casually. He thought: how a man without a woman is silenced, how cold food makes a hermit. A woman without a man—well, they had no such capacity for solitude. Look at Abby Joslin, her lilac-scented afternoons with Buck Herman. Or they were schoolteachers and social seamstresses. A spinster quilt stowed in the closet of anyone who had ever endured an illness.

Once in the decade that had now been marked by the men's arrival to Abbott's, Mrs. Heald had mended Abbott's clothing. How she ever got those shirts, a pair of wool trousers, off of him Heald had not an idea, but she had filled the washtub with boiling water where she only used cold for themselves and she sat up two nights with the click-click of the thimble. He saw the work had held well. He would tell Mrs. Heald. He thought then, would he have had the stomach to come up had not the clothes been once washed and mended?

They set to task—at least to gauge the ruin of the house, could they build anew upon the old foundation?—and Abbott stood back in the rubble of his own mother's rose garden (roses lost to the fire) until it was high noon and then he bowed his head and joined them.

By midafternoon the men began to sprinkle their work with a few words and Giddens recalled the eighties when there were spell-downs hosted by schoolhouse No. 6 on alternating Saturdays and boys came from surrounding towns as contestants for such high jinks and high spirits. "Refreshments served by our mothers were second to none," added Herman.

"I recall Abbott was a winner," said Giddens slyly. Abbott bent his head to hide an inclination.

"Prize money of a half-dollar and a pie in a basket to sweeten your mother!" called Tuttle.

"I was a winner," Abbott said finally. "You'll remember we boarded the schoolmaster."

"Why, you cheated!" Giddens brought levity and a fine mood of friendship. The men did not laugh aloud but their eyes creased and they straightened their backs in mock incredulity.

The postman held his tongue for his conversation lacked practice. He knew Abbott's son had no desire for the farm—a joyless boyhood without a mother. There had been a letter—but he had deemed it better for old Abbott to retain his hope. He had heard Abbott say, "My son will be home one day and we'll rake this place back into the running."

Abbott's hope would keep the other men at bay, although Heald did not know who among them could afford to pay off the back taxes.

He didn't want the farm for himself—only that he was a preservationist. Or, as if the Heald-Abbott lands put together again would recall time from the store of the last century. Willard Heald believed such a thing could be done; that there were caches of time stowed, say, at a defunct field's blurring edges. If you could grasp them in two hands, hold them hard to you, you might use them to stop that other flow. Like digging out a pond in the course of a river.

By late afternoon they had a frame up for a tool-shed—Abbott said a man living alone didn't need a house, proper, and it was the things of wood and steel that were worse off for the weather. None of the men protested.

It was time to go home to supper and Heald broke off from the crew. "Show us inside your lean-to, then, Abbott. If it's not so rank as it looks." It was meant in part for a joke and taken as such; Frank Abbott acquiesced with a half-smile and the men stooped and followed Heald.

Abbott came behind them, his frame blocking any filtered daylight. Did he stand plugging up the doorway for a moment too long, as if to frighten them? Heald thought, it's the way a spider would show you his home if his home were not a few dust-gathering threads in the rafters. Heald saw the others were afraid as they had not been since the sad stringy ends of their childhoods.

Had any of them ever seen a place where a man lived without a woman?

It was cavelike, the warmth of the center of the Earth, a settler boy's dream of last century's Indian dwelling. A fire pit glowed with smokeless embers in the center of a stone circle.

The dirt floor was covered with burlap; over that a dozen home-cured sheepskins had been laid out so that there was the redolence of lanolin mixed with mint hanging in bundles as big as mooseheads mounted on the walls. The bed was a bank of hay bales covered in old blankets.

"A man would think you were a primitive," said Tuttle.

No one else spoke. They felt each other's breathing, the teepee was a lung, an old stomach. Heald reached for the shoulder of the neighbor. Abbott's shoulder did not give way and so the postman removed his hand rather mechanically. But Abbott was trembling before he broke the silence.

His voice was too high and Heald knew that each man would willingly forget it. Or did that narrow voice recall to them their own boyhoods, before they had known love, or any semblance of it?

"The farm goes to my boy," said Abbott. "Are there laws say no man shall share another's happiness? Well that is why our forefathers chose New Hampshire.

"I shall not part with it, not an acre. The man who gets my land will also get my dead body."

The men broke off singly. Abbott's sheep had herded themselves near the lean-to and he moved about with purpose to get grain in buckets and water in the trough. It was just a short walk down the hill for Heald.

III

"Do you know, Willard," said Mrs. Heald, "when Margaret Abbott left I imagined for half a night I could depart also."

"You were in consultation?"

"Oh no. We were never more than neighbors."

"I suppose she had her reason."

"Would you have turned wild like Abbott?"

So this was what she wanted to know. Or would he be the same man without her. And then it occurred to him she had said all this before—perhaps she said it every evening. And for a response he always read aloud while she worked away at her collages. Tonight it was a stretch of needlework— Woman's currency, he thought, her hands in motion.

"The girl Frances Giddens has been after me about some letters." He startled at the sound of his own voice and readjusted his spectacles rather compulsively.

"Ah," Mrs. Heald noted mildly.

"Indeed I wish she'd leave me be." Was he indignant? Hah, it was only his wife. But the line that hung loosely between them was taut now and if either one had thought to pluck it like a stringed instrument it would have sounded out of tune.

"Abbott has made himself a proper home amidst that fire rubble you women have despaired of," he went on after a while.

"A resilient fellow."

"We're all resilient here."

"Who will he sell to?"

"He'll make a go of it."

"He can't possibly."

She infuriated him. She would have left him.

The sun sank latest in June but deeply into itself, with great finality. The winter had stamped their bones and now they were through with it and Frank Abbott had passed it sleeping by an open fire.

It seemed to him they no longer spoke freely, each for fear of losing ground to the other. They shared no laughter, only domestic injury. Now he had struck up a surprising friendship with the Giddens girl—he musn't pretend in his own head that he didn't know her name and call her that, Frances—and there was no thought of losing ground to her because they only met in the out-of-doors where the ground beneath their feet belonged to neither.

"Why Willard," said his wife. "Did we have new residents last year?"

"We did not."

"And the year before?"

"No one had applied to be."

She rose from the table.

The sky was sharp as a scythe in spring and he set out wearing no overcoat but gross-grain leather boots freshly oiled. He left the house by crossing the adjacent pasture and then up through a stretch of woods earmarked for a bit of logging in the next year or so. He preferred to avoid the roads lately. In any case, walking through the forest at this time of year was to be in God's graces. Of course he wondered how early in the day the young Giddens girl would take the hidden trails but he put this thought aside for it was always such pleasure when she surprised him.

He could reach Main Street in half an hour at a brisk pace, in time to avoid altogether the meager morning traffic of Main Street.

Lately Willard Heald had received uncloaked offers from city addresses to buy a farmer out of delinquency, pay off back taxes to acquire a summer home cheaply. If these prospectors were not those who also summered they sent along letters of recommendation from those who had.

And there had been a handful of city people who arrived in person, knocked on doors, paced the boundaries along rambling stone walls, a stand of pine or maple. They were loud in the woods and they chose difficult routes boggy or steep and if they became mired they shouted continuously until some farmer could stand the noise no longer, reluctantly left his chore to aid them. Heald had heard them cursing fiercely over a twisted ankle.

It took all of an hour to sort the mail and he hoisted his bag over his shoulders (for Mrs. Heald had made a regular contraption complete with straps and belt) and stepped out onto Main Street to commence delivery.

There they were: city people with well-collared necks, a man and a woman who had already stayed a night for how else could they have arrived so early?

It was only June, he thought. They usually preyed on Garner in September or October. But this couple looked well-fed and as if they thought nothing of conquering a farmstead. He strode toward them.

"Are you lost, then?" he called out.

"Oh," said the woman. "I do believe we've just become your neighbors.

"He said it was a postman next door, didn't he, Hal?"

So the hermit had betrayed them.

IV

The Bickleys arrived bearing money the color and tang of Hal Bickley's childhood lawn that sloped down to the Hudson. Heald felt insouciance in his handshake and his gait betrayed he was a consummate automobile rider.

He was deaf in one ear and it was with no small mortification one was forced to speak louder. ("Must we shout as if in crude anger?" said Tuttle who had never raised his voice, even above his sawmill.) Bickley's hair was a mahogany color and some of those who subscribed to a periodical claimed to have pinpointed the bottle.

There was a rumor he was a bank man (they dug their savings underground. A bank in Saskoba Falls or Manchester—well it was only crooks collected interest) but Bickley's new bills might well have been folded into paper airplanes, so inconsequential they seemed to the gut of the transaction. Bickley said tritely that he could see future generations (he was in his thirties—the hearing loss from a childhood illness with a long convalescence) spring forth from the granite seeded fields of New Hampshire.

"Do you mean to farm, then?"

"It may be a hobby," Bickley shouted. "I'll consult you should my interest fall that way."

Men who were hushed at the drop of a hat—well now they were deeply silenced. Hal Bickley in a black overcoat of so fine a make that its thin, supple fabric reflected no light.

But it was Vivian Bickley, dark and gold as a burnt-oak barrel, refined and yet impulsive, who chose Garner. They had studied a map of New England, she told Mrs. Heald, the place they were all from, really, she laughed, and first she chose New Hampshire because it looked like a sail and then she chose Garner because it was a sail within a sail.

They had wanted to turn the paper money into something with dignity and weight, she said, and this pleased Mrs. Heald more perhaps than it should have.

How could he have missed them? They'd been in Garner three days already. But Heald had been crossing the forests and they'd driven the roads. He imagined the dust their large automobile had kicked up. He imagined their arrival, a first stop at Maude's on Main Street. Bickley would have taken off his hat at the threshold; both stretched their legs discreetly to hide that the drive from New York had been more than eight hours. The inside of the store was dark and wood-smelling. The sound of flies, the bell on the door. At first, all they could see were the eyes of Buck Herman the proprietor glowing like cat eyes at night. Then he became a silhouette, then he was filled in and he was a troll, a truncated man, no eyebrows, hunched behind the long glass-topped counter like he'd been there since the beginning of time. Vivian Bickley stood a pace behind her husband, Willard Heald imagined.

"We're looking to buy some land," Hal Bickley must have said, loudly. "Maybe an old farm. We have money the color of the best lawns on the Eastern Seaboard. One of us is broad-shouldered and the other is slim but fertile. (Willard winced.) What have you got there: chocolate?

peppermint? We'll take a couple of cups of coffee off the pot. What can you tell us for that?"

Buck Herman the romantic. The postman could easily write his script: "Well then you, Young Lady Hanging Back, you look like you might be librarian material and you, Young Man Who Knows the Upholstery of Automobiles, do you know something of the engines too? Why not. Your children will be born here."

(Although this was sentimental, Heald corrected himself: the Bickley woman had not the curvature of spine or the love of quiet old things to be a librarian. They would have to find someone else or give the leather-bound collections to the Saskoba Public Library.)

"Abbott owes back taxes," Herman might have said. "Thirty years. No one knows but me and I haven't the stomach to deliver such humiliation.

"He has a son who could take him." He added the sweets on a scrap of paper, handing proof of his careful addition with its tiny sum to Mrs. Bickley.

Oh no, not necessary, the city woman mimed, to show they came in peace.

Willard knew what the Bickleys saw: old man with moldy suspenders and yellowed undershirt, wool pants as if Revolutionary War issue, albeit well-mended. Fields pocked with milkweed and poison ivy, fences like grandfathers' teeth, caught with old wet wool. Goldenrod growing in strong. Forty acres would sound like a lot to such folk—a kingdom, the woman would whisper. The house was mostly gone to fire, but the barn, weathered to silvery gray, would strike their fancy with its Pegasus weathervane. Abbott's father had bent it in the forge in another century.

They would salvage tapered beams. Swallows in Heald's kitchen this year so imagine how they made their mud nests at Abbott's. Small talk to get the old hermit talking.

If Buck Herman felt guilty he didn't show it. But then he was a public figure when stationed behind his counter and such men were exempt from guilt altogether. The coffee was burnt and tarry.

Late in the day, Abbott came down to the store bearing his money. Herman had an old cigar box in which he could keep it. A few men were there, Giddens who had a good hand in building the toolshed. Heald stepped forward.

"They're letting him stay on," said Heald. "They've shaved an acre at the edge, a veritable haven. We'll all pitch in to raise a good clapboard."

"It's not a site for a house," voiced someone.

"Have you a better acre on your land for new construction?" Heald addressed them all.

"Abbott gets a new house while the newcomers acquire an old ruin," said Buck Herman philosophically. "It's the summer of 1925, by golly."

When the traveling dowser with his rods at his hip and particularly weighted pendant came a week before the well-digger, the men gathered to watch the pendulum draw circles above an underground spring, keen as ever to a farm's hidden source of water.

It was a month after Frank Abbott had been installed in the new place with the superfluous bedroom (Willard had sided with him but been outvoted. Why would an old man need a wall to separate himself?) that the postman had a letter from him to the Bickley's campsite. Vivian Bickley came to greet him from the open hallways, labyrinth of construction. He handed her the envelope—Abbott's blocky letters punished the paper, and she looked up at him judiciously and said, "It must have been painful to write the name of another man above the address one feels to be one's own."

(Willard could recall Abbott had been clumsy in penmanship as a fellow schoolboy. Master Denton with his great soft paw over the boy's hand—already work-hardened—drawing out the script in swoops and curls, a deft rhythm.)

In one place the pen had ripped into the letter. She read it on the spot, standing up, and Heald felt he hadn't been dismissed and so he stood beside her.

Might I come up to the old place? I fear it has already changed so much. If I could buy it back I would but it's in such a condition that the bank will not mortgage it. I inquired.

Let it be known that this will always be my home.

And his name there the same as it had been in a schoolboy's swerving hand.

"We've been told by the insurance man that the barn should be razed," said Vivian drily.

"I never let the insurance man onto my land," said Heald.

"Franklin Abbott used the basement for household garbage. We had to have the Maynard Fire Department up here, Mr. Heald. To hose it down, bleach it, monitor the wood stove. It took a week to dry the whole mess out. If you knew your mushrooms you'd have been in business. It cost us a fortune." As if Abbott was his responsibility.

"There's a fine stone arch in that basement," said Heald. "The way they used to build a foundation."

"Yes," said Vivian. "My husband pointed it out to me. He's too tall to stand beneath it."

"The house wasn't built for him, you know." Heald picked up his mailbag and turned to go.

⚜

Willard Heald had only to see the back of the man: Hal Bickley's scornful exit from the store on a Saturday morning, to know he had found Abbott's old foaling shed.

Heald imagined that now Hal Bickley felt sure of the place as he felt sure of a lover. The coaxing it out, early gifts of new plow and timber, the twenty-inch pine boards Heald had noticed were salvaged.

"Trees don't grow like that anymore," Hal Bickley must have said to Buck Herman.

(No, thought Willard. The girth of another era.)

Even the hayloft that smelled of cat piss must sing its gratitude to be cared for by Hal Bickley.

("Let it be, Willard," said his wife disgustedly.

("New residents must take care to be in accordance!"

("You won't go so far as to do anything in public," she said, as if a softer amendment.

("A public figure stands in the center of his circle. I am a man of circumferences, Mrs. Heald. I watch over the far borders.")

One day Hal Bickley instead of his wife came out to receive the mail and he said to Heald, as casually as he could muster, "Do you know there's an old foaling shed on the north side that wasn't in the deed. Fancy that. Seems Abbott must have forgotten it existed."

Heald was silent and this silence seemed to incite something in Bickley.

"I figure if I was leaving the only home I ever knew, boy I'd know about an old foaling shed. I'd charge double for it. I'd mourn it," he laughed loudly and ironically. "Best-kept building on the place, too. Good roof'll last another fifty. Boy I'd chain myself to that foaling shed before I let some city folk pay off my back taxes."

Heald was still silent.

"What's in the Ordinances about these old maples?" he waved his long arm at the yard, changing the subject. "I've had a forester up from Boston."

"What does a Bostoner know of forest?"

"Call him an expert, then. He says better to clear them out before they go of their own accord with lightning or snowfall."

"Ask Buck Herman."

"What does a storekeeper know about forestry, Mr. Heald?"

When Willard Heald walked away he imagined the man called after him, a derisive echo, "Will our children be natives, then, Mr. Heald? Like you, Herman, Abbott? Is there some kind of birthright?

"For the daughter I'll turn that shed into a playhouse with miniatures of everything her little heart desires."

"How did you know it was a foaling shed?" said Heald at another visit.

"I suppose one of the local boys told me what it was used for," said Bickley absently.

The boy Asa Robinson told Heald that the Bickleys found a wasps' nest in the el of the old summer kitchen and hired him to do away with it. Mrs. Bickley came out to watch—"Don't you kill any of those creatures, young man."

"Look at them," she whispered. "Prancing fanatics."

"City folk can afford to care for nature," the postman told Asa.

"Nature?" he said.

"All that's green, and the animals."

"They'll just move on to warmer quarters," said the boy. "Between the walls of their new farmhouse. But I didn't kill a one, just like she told me."

"They'll be swaggering or stumbling like sleepy colts from the woodwork come November," said Heald. "The color of brown glass, aren't they. Bladed eyebrows and the ability to resurrect themselves." For in his time he had also noticed nature.

Asa Robinson was silent and Heald shook himself. "No," he said sharply. "The man Hal Bickley will step on the one losing the midmorning battle and scuff it toward the edge of the room just like the rest of us."

The boy looked level at him with some wonder. "That is what we do, Mr. Heald, isn't it."

Part Four
Abbott's Return

I

In an every day sort of way Mrs. Heald saw herself through the eyes of the town—as if the postmaster's wife were public property. But inside she knew her fears to be exotic.

She feared that as a childless woman she was not trusted by other women.

She feared automobiles but if she made this fear known her husband would raise his voice ever so slightly: "Rationality is what is called for, Mrs. Heald." They would go for a drive with young Asa Robinson during which her husband, beside her, would be as white-knuckled as a barn owl.

She did not write things down as her husband did; if her life were a glass bottle she had reached the skinny neck of it. Childlessness had another meaning: we subscribe to a grim future.

New England had always been agreeable toward its spinsters. Even the name sounded of productivity, a drop spindle and wool carders in nimble hands. Mrs. Heald personally believed in witches, but the Twentieth Century had simply denied them and if there were relics they lived in cities.

Garner was three hundred souls, smaller than Maynard, Westborough; by far Saskoba, but all the schoolteachers in Tewksboro County were Garner women and necessarily childless. There were others too, she could count them on two hands, some married like herself, none of the constitution to make talk of it. All did fine handwork, all were dutiful volunteers, and yet she was close to none of them. (Although she took pains to reserve judgment of Abby Joslin. She remembered the fly-by-night Passarro. She remembered Abigail fetched back from where she'd run after him and then the grief that people said was unwarranted, was as if he'd been a son and soldier instead of a wolf-in-sheep's-clothing in a time of peace.) It seemed to Mrs. Heald each spinster had a sister with children or a neighbor who needed help with the littlest—had sought out a surrogate family and listened to the mother's trials with infinite and bitter patience. Among those listeners were:

Lucinda Leary
Grace Weston
Abby Joslin

She had been in school with all three. Were they barren even then or did they swing their braids the same as the brood mares?

Lucinda, Sarah Leary's sister, was a schoolteacher herself; hair the color of a Christmas pomegranate shipped in tissue and held at Heald's tidy post office for the addressee to pick up himself. (A mailman couldn't be expected to make his rounds carrying a box of fruit ripened to perfection.) Two schoolgirl braids had gradually become one long rope down a narrow back as if a drunkard sobered at the sight of her.

Mrs. Heald (Columbine Mason. What a worthless name it had turned out to be) and Lucinda and Sarah Leary, traveling unchaperoned, had passed an entire summer in the nation's capital in the study of government history. It was a course for young women that they should be better suited to listen to the matters that engaged their husbands and offer if not a word of advice then at least an intelligence of gaze that should make proud any man of the Twentieth Century.

Mrs. Heald remembered nothing of government history. She saw in her mind's eye instead: morning; the glossy-headed girl who was her younger self crossing the front hall of the eminent house in which the three girls boarded. Suddenly through the slice of polished brass in the front door shot one, two, three envelopes in crisp white uniforms.

(And stars were bright as brass in her girlhood, she thought, on a clear night in October, the first killing frost, when you hauled in bushels of green tomatoes.)

Before she could stop herself she had reached down to scoop up the pile. She remembered the cool marble checkerboard as if the foyer of a grand hotel.

There was one envelope that bore her name—deep purple with a faint tea gold around the edge of each studied letter.

It was the dark brew of a poisonous berry they used, and India tea to fix the ink without bleeding. Her mother's pen was square nibbed, a stolid, feminine personage.

Lucinda had looked at the letter: "But we'll be home in a week. You don't miss your mother?" Certainly one would never have children if one had never missed one's mother.

Grace Weston—well, she'd go through them all in an effort to understand it. Grace had married Armand

Derbyshire from the "gold coast" of Garner. Her sister-in-law's layette had been passed along at a ladies tea not a month after her wedding. It was a trunk full of trifles, really, all the useful things used through. Grace's sister-in-law had added some pear soap wrapped in Chinese paper that was known to be gentle on a baby's skin and somehow the smell of it—spicy, a bit like a store-bought carnation—clung to Grace even now, some thirty years later.

Dozens of first pregnancies were lost for modesty. The corset too tight, the housework exhausting, the appetite weakened so that the man bellowed about the waste in his house and the woman simply stopped preparing her own portion.

A woman must hide her pregnancy for a man's sensibilities. Then one day she cradled an impeccable bundle and she passed it to her husband as they entered the church and a gentle reverence was inspired in all the congregation.

Grace Weston Derbyshire bowed her head: "Who knows how a child would survive in the Twentieth Century?" She passed the layette to Abby Joslin. Mrs. Heald could not remember exactly: was it before or after Passarro?

The walk from Abby Joslin's would take an hour and the wings of the forest darkened quickly and the chill pressed her arms to her body. Mrs. Heald looked forward to taking a stance against the cold. Lavender and mauve—she had always fancied the sunset was for women (dinner would be served without fail into the eternity she imagined) and the sunrise for the menfolk. Her husband had beat the sun out of the house every day of their marriage. Once, a long time ago, when they still thought to conceive a child, he told her the greatest relief was in the morning. He had tucked two hard-boiled eggs into a patch pocket.

The clouds were undeniably the color of slate and Mrs. Heald took a wool kerchief and tied it round her ears. She had a large head and hair like a thicket that would not fit beneath any hat.

(She had suffered an almost constant earache through the winter. Even in June, her hearing was still shy as a barn kitten.)

They had drawn the same tracks as children. Sometimes Abby had joined her—two solemn girls making their way unseen from one farm to another. But there was no great divide from the far side of which she looked down upon her own girlhood. She had become a woman rather privately, in the off hours, in stillness.

As to the future she was shortsighted and she viewed this quality in the childless Abby Joslin as well.

("If we had our own Hester Prynne we would be famous," said Willard. "But don't go exalting Abby Joslin. Besides, do you think Herman would go there were it not for the lilacs?")

"It's a lovely dusk, Abby. If you won't let me in at least come out for a while."

"Be on your way or you'll be forced to an awkward encounter."

"Put him off and let me come in a while. I've walked such a way. I need a word with you about Willard."

Abigail laughed at full throttle. "The postman doesn't come here, Columbine."

"Oh, no; I didn't mean—"

"Shall I have to shock you to get you off my doorstep?"

"I am not shocked by Buck Herman's needs of the flesh."

"But mine?" Abby painted her brows, the only woman in the whole of New England. Mrs. Heald had been only once to Boston.

"Abby! Why don't you allow him to marry you?"

"What a reasonable woman!"

"Well you're not getting any younger."

She almost snorted, then raised a hand to the figure beyond Mrs. Heald taking shape from dusk's crosshatch.

❧•☙

Whatever should transpire during a day—the men and the women going their separate ways—the evening was what one married for. There they were again. The table was pine but well made. It was a curiosity, really: years ago Mrs. Heald had painted upon its honeyed surface a colorful map of the United States of America. Each state was precisely delineated with lakes of note, mountain ranges, and rivers. She had begun on the East Coast to mark in capital cities, secondary cities, and population numbers, but her husband had projected a weary disapproval. As it was early in the marriage (one year? three?), Mrs. Heald forgave him and said to herself proudly that he saw enough of the names of America's cities as the postmaster.

She had wanted a map on the wall so that she could study geography while bound to the kitchen by some chore.

Willard said there was no need to adorn one's home; she should pay full heed to a chore and she was permitted to learn any subject from a book in the long evenings.

How she had loved the names: Taos, Toledo, Topeka. There was a thin spot in the tablecloth over Nevada. The breadboard sat in the west and rubbed the linen through to the deserts of Nevada. The map was always covered over ("Let us have our meals in peace, Mrs. Heald") unless there were children in the house to whom one or the other of the old couple could deliver an impromptu lesson.

She looked at him and she did not know what he was thinking.

An unexpected anger rose in her gorge. "Why did you prevent me from finishing my map, Willard?" she burst in suddenly.

"Prevent you?" She had startled him.

"Why yes; I had even measured all the lines in pencil for the printing of the names of cities."

"The weather had worsened and there were socks to be darned and mended."

It was true. The table was meant to be a summer project but it had been more tedious than she had anticipated and she decided to paint each state a different color just as the atlas from which she'd copied it. The noxious oily smell permeated the house once the windows were closed in September and both of them had lost their appetites entirely by October. Her husband was right—it had been a practical consideration.

II

"If you put up the fruits of the forest," Mrs. Heald instructed Vivian Bickley, "you may add a richness to many a soup throughout the winter."

"Do you mean mushrooms?" said the younger woman, determined to prove herself a quick learner.

"Of all sorts and the tinsel herb that grows in spates beneath the mosses. Even pine needles will do when you've no other seasoning; black birch and nettle for steeps and poultices."

"Witchcraft!" cried Vivian, laughing.

"How else would one come through the winter?"

Mrs. Heald heard the clatter of seasons: torpor of spring, fall with its russet-cloaked pallbearers, winter— dazzling, deathly.

The two women cut through the Bickley's north field past the foaling shed to get to the rich woods where Mrs. Heald knew there to be mushrooms. "Do you know our mascot, the White Pine?" she asked. Mrs. Heald imagined, as she had since girlhood, an aerial view from the high rush-green crown and a terrestrial watch like a seismograph.

In July, the White Pine's leader was new green and smelled of bitter lime.

They wore long skirts with aprons and men's boots that Mrs. Heald had provided. Her thick gray hair was packed in a white kerchief. Vivian Bickley kept up easily with the strides but was careful to walk behind her guide. Mrs. Heald felt it.

She had crossed her husband deliberately. "We shall not befriend those who stole from our lifelong neighbor," said Willard.

"It seems to me they may have done him a service." She wasn't sure she believed this entirely. She had been raised to believe in hard work and quiet evenings. She wasn't really a farm wife but she used her own legs to go from one place to another and it was she who split logs into slender quarters and some thin as matchsticks for kindling. Willard sharpened the axe.

This woman was the age a daughter of hers might have been. Mrs. Heald rolled out a simple pie of potatoes and onions, nothing Willard would miss, had he been counting.

She had started out then turned back then started out and diverted but finally she had gone calling.

"I hope I'm not usurping the place of a friend who usually joins you on these outings," Vivian said at length.

"Going for mushrooms is a solitary venture," said Mrs. Heald.

"Oh, dear, I'm intruding then!"

They were walking in single file. She wished she had taken along some of her own dried fruit leather. She would like to hand back a small offering.

"You've certainly traveled a stretch of the imagination to settle in Garner, Mrs. Bickley," Mrs. Heald offered instead, without turning or stopping.

"Do call me Vivian."

"I shall." She waited a long beat. "But *my* Christian

name suits me no longer," she finished, pensive, or as if to prolong the conversation.

"I'm sorry," said Vivian, haltingly, after several moments of tromping. "May I complain for a moment? The woods don't hold it against me—it's hard to see that anything you say matters with so few people around to listen."

"The trees have their intelligence."

Vivian said nothing while the forest thickened around them. Mrs. Heald thought, they would wait for mushrooms.

They could get all the way to Main Street in this direction. Into the sun at noonday, south, and it was a long swath of young oak to follow. Then when they heard the rumble of one or two motorcars starting up their engines the newcomer would be deafened by the clap of civilization.

"Mrs. Heald?" Vivian queried as if her guide had disappeared suddenly.

"We'll do without our gathering for today. We'll accustom you to woods-walking."

They came to a track with a ridge of weeds growing down the spine like the fur of a dog raised in fear. After the unordered forest, Mrs. Heald could sense Vivian's attempt to align herself with this man-made trail. A road to nowhere in the middle of the forest. The women sat on a log at the edge and rested, watching the track as though it were a river—a worthy place to lay the gaze.

They had brought neither food nor water and after swinging the arms for an hour the hands felt stunned and empty. The woods hummed around them.

She didn't wish it but any flights of fancy she might have taken were robbed by concern of her husband. *Summer's here,* she'd caught his slanting script. Summer's here. Summer should have been exiled from Garner with the indolent Tories. It was something her husband would say. But the handwriting was a wilderness pressing up against the printed columns of the newspaper. She read:

> I had vowed against it, but by the time summer came I had forgotten entirely March, even cold-footed April. Good-bye to cocoons and catkins! By the time summer came why summer was already upon us and we were crazy for it and had thrown all precaution to the wind like an idiotic, open-faced baby with damp hands grinning toothlessly for whatever the weather had to offer. If it rained on his soft head well then he grinned and tomorrow thrice as many cucumbers.

He was at the mercy of the season, careless with it, she had caught him trembling as he fastened the buttons of his trousers. She, Columbine Heald, did not even cultivate cucumbers. Had never. The postman disliked pickles.

Mrs. Heald rose abruptly.

"Shall we go along the road for a while?" said Vivian from behind her.

The track led a mile through the forest. At the end, in a small clearing that seemed to have no particular reason, was the old Poor Farm, last home to the family Miller. Where had they gone, Vivian wanted to know, and Mrs. Heald replied that they had not been from Garner anyway, so went to join their people thirty miles west in Keene or thereabouts where, strangely enough, the gardens bloomed a full two weeks earlier.

Mrs. Heald found herself shocked by such a pale thumbprint of human life in the midst of the teeming forest. But she pointed out bee balm in the deserted garden; mint that came up and, unchecked, spread its pungent roots into such a thick lace that the mole was twice blinded. There was dill, self-seeded, and the muddy husks of last year's swallow nests, horsehair woven in, she noticed.

"Newcomers make one feel old before one's time, Vivian," said Mrs. Heald.

She must shake herself free of the doubts she had about her husband. She pointed out the windbreak of White Pines, the northern quarter. "Do you remember the whistle of a rare glass bottle?" said Mrs. Heald with forced gaiety. But it was true. Up came a wonderful sound. "It is not unlike the sound of the White Pine whistling."

She hadn't meant it whimsically but she saw that Vivian took it so for perhaps blowing across the mouth of a bottle wasn't something that was done in a more recent childhood. She let it be. It was enough that an afternoon outing should yield a lightening between them; and that the newcomer could identify the White Pine.

"Why weren't we shown this place when we were in the buying market?" cried Vivian. "You must have laughed at us, bearing wads of cash, green as our money. But this place would have suited us, and we wouldn't have poor Mr. Abbott to haunt us."

"Well we might at least have made an offer. Who owns it?"

Mrs. Heald said, "You'll buy out the whole town of Garner."

"My husband says it could use diversification," Vivian laughed.

"Yes," said Mrs. Heald, as if agreeing. "But you have yet to see an autumn."

"Oh Mrs. Heald, you underestimate us!" Vivian was still laughing. "Besides, consider our latitude. We're yet south of merry old England!"

Vivian was picking mint and greedily stuffing it into her overstitched skirt pocket.

"It's a weed," called Mrs. Heald.

Vivian raised her head. "A better souvenir than nothing!"

There was new eagerness in Vivian's step on the way home. She would tell her husband she'd discovered the Poor Farm with its peppermint garden. The two of them would gloat over it and then be disappointed—there was an easement on it. She left Vivian off and made her way back down the hill to her own dwelling.

Her husband was already in the doorway. "No mushrooms?" he greeted her.

"The Bickley woman fancied the mint from the Poor Farm garden."

"You've made your acquaintances."

He did not seem to remember he'd forbade it.

It was easy to find an excuse to pass a morning with the new neighbor. She was an apt listener, tall but without a queen's bearing. And easy to forgive her for her fancy ideas about Frank Abbott's half-burned farmhouse because she painstakingly laid out what was practical and Mrs. Heald saw great inventions spring from the explication. The Heald home was the last in Garner to earn its indoor plumbing.

Mrs. Heald had never thought of herself as a friendly woman but maybe she was. She had patted Vivian's arm and surprised herself. It was a trifle, really—the younger woman upset by the lack of some private supply in Maude's Penny Candy—and Mrs. Heald had said wisely, "It's a store owned by a man, Vivian. Inquire of the Giddens boarders." And instead of taking her advice, Vivian had countered with spirit Mrs. Heald couldn't help admiring,

"Well how do you manage?"

Indeed it was curious that Vivian did not make the acquaintance of the female summer boarders—three stylish young women whom even Mrs. Heald began, from afar, to fancy. There was one all whitest milk and honey who seemed to have a way with Frances Giddens. Mrs. Heald's heart lifted, for then the postman would stay well clear of her.

"We are three strange households on Abbott Road this summer," she remarked to Vivian Bickley.

"But we're four! Don't forget the man for whom our road is christened!"

The younger woman came to call on Mrs. Heald several mornings each week, dressed rather too elaborately for the small, dark kitchen with its constant pine box of seedlings on the high windowsill (no matter what the season).

Vivian confessed she wasn't wanted around the new house anyhow. "Not a man but my husband has addressed me since we arrived in Garner. And yours," she said rather too thoughtfully for Mrs. Heald's comfort.

"No," said Mrs. Heald. "You shouldn't expect it."

Beyond the drying of the Poor Farm mint Vivian had shown herself disinterested in domicile pastimes so the talk was purely for company. There were no recipes exchanged, little gossip (for Vivian was acquainted with no one). Mrs. Heald realized with a harrowing pressure in her abdomen that this was why one had a daughter.

Also that the new neighbor took her mind away from Willard. She was full with premonition.

⥽ III ⥼

Once Vivian came in the afternoon. Mrs. Heald stiffened at the knock on the door. Odd, she thought later, that I should think for a moment that my husband knocked at his own kitchen door.

They had been that morning to the Maynard Pit, said Vivian. Had Mrs. Heald ever accompanied her husband?

Mrs. Heald thought, it wasn't the destination that had so charmed Vivian but that she had been out with her husband. The country woman inquired, "Did you go out often then in the city, Vivian?"

Of course they had. "There wasn't a house to be built," Vivian replied shortly.

"Well you're ahead of me, then," said Mrs. Heald. "My husband has never found a reason to visit the Maynard Pit and as he is on the road through the week it's not travel he wants on Sunday."

"Oh, but we passed the postman out of Maynard this very morning," said Vivian. "Not a quarter-mile from the Pit. We stopped. He waved us on most sternly."

"My husband has no route in Maynard."

"We didn't mistake him."

"Indeed." Mrs. Heald found herself flustered. But why should she be apprised of Willard's whereabouts? "It's a warm day. I've no refreshments." She had never before turned this guest away.

"I shan't stay. But it seems all of Garner had been today to the neighboring hamlet. You'll not believe whom we escorted!"

"Well then who else did you find along the way."

"Why, Frances Giddens and the red-haired gentleman boarder. Along for a stroll, mightily surprised to see us."

"I certainly missed an adventure," Mrs. Heald said tightly.

"He's a charming fellow, actually. Robert Yates—and lives not five blocks from our old apartment. Once I glanced back, Mrs. Heald, and the girl had her hand open as if she wished it to be taken."

"I shouldn't read too much into it. A girl like that will never marry."

⧉•⧉

Let me tell you about November, Vivian Bickley. It is dark at four-thirty on the crest of Abbott Road for the shadow of Hunter's Hill leans with the weight of the sky behind it.

As a girl, Mrs. Heald had imagined dusk rolled out like a carpet. Dusk from a cave in Hunter's Hill. A gray toad from that cave rode upon her back. She could reach around to stroke it.

There are secrets held aloft. The way the light takes leave like a ghost nurse. Lifts off slate-roofed houses. Windows with wavy glass. You will learn to pinch the curtains in along the baseboard, Vivian.

As a girl she was never cold, for, her father said, You were born here. As native to the road as the long shadows. Visible in dusk and then woven into the night; only the cut of her breathing to warn the world she passed through.

In November the evenings are longer than the days. A long string of evenings that come after one another like Indian war boats, hollowed logs silently drifting downstream, a nation on the waters. As a child she didn't mind that winter was coming.

Most of the trees along the road are White Pines, Vivian. Or dark puppets of White Pines folded into the ribs of dusk. Soft wood, soft heart, cheap, easily marked and dented. More rocks in the fields in New Hampshire than in Vermont and fewer sugar maples. Not a frontier like Maine, weathered and wrinkled and salt-welted as a farmer's hand, without Boston, without much shorefront, mean in November.

Dusk holds the girl, forever mid-slope, as if she were a penitent of the underworld, carrying water in a sieve. It is not that she was too young or too slender to reach the top; she was a strong child, short legs, broad shoulders, never cold, kindly allowing creatures a ride upon her back. In memory such a girl is left forever climbing.

In the west the night lifts the day off her feet before the day has even put her slippered feet down. White skirts, black skirts, pale feet, dust flying.

—⊱•⊰—

No sooner had Vivian left than the postman returned, dusk not far behind him. It frightened Mrs. Heald just a bit, this near-collision of her company and her husband. He paused as if to unnerve her, kept his boots on and crossed the kitchen.

"Ah. You've made a friend, Mrs. Heald. A friend in fair weather."

"She'll see the winter through."

"I think not. Thin-blooded."

"You've had a hike today, Willard."

"My accustomary."

"You were seen all the way to Maynard."

"Was I?"

"You might have taken a ride. To be home sooner."

He was sour of spirits. Couldn't walk so far as he used to, thought Mrs. Heald.

"What did I tell you. I am a man of the perimeters."

"Well the summer folk have a right to see our countryside."

"Ah, then, Mrs. Bickley must have passed them."

"Frances Giddens and the young man had the sense to ride home in an automobile. You're tired, Willard."

"I've come home for my simple supper."

It would be so forever, thought Mrs. Heald. She moved to the stove where the simple supper awaited, served two portions. She turned with grace and it was as if the table had been laid without her. Of its own accord, night unfolded.

They lay down together. His boots were clustered neatly by the closet, her things upon a chair placed modestly for that purpose. Talk had ceased since they left the kitchen. It was one night in a hundred they lay down together. As if on this night neither had strength to repel it. She could watch his face without looking. Blackish concavities for eyes—had there ever been a time he shut them before her? She waited for the ease of the full bed around her, his restive motions of re-dressing. He would put his boots on in the kitchen. It wouldn't be long now.

As a child she had stayed out as long as possible. She could still tune her ear to her mother's voice calling her for dinner. There it was. Singeing the cold air as it traveled. She would receive it with its edges sparking; it would cover up the last small rustlings of the swallowed-in-dusk world.

She would warn Vivian tomorrow: the road will soon be selvaged with ice fossils and the ugly frozen fur of an animal. Fault lines from before you were born, Vivian Bickley, bleeding arctic dust, all earth a rock, a hard calling, the absence of birds, a silence that can't be punctured, sky as dull as lead, a silence that you're certain you weren't born for.

He was in the kitchen. They had electric lights there but he never used them. She moved her cramped body to the center of the bed.

She could give in now completely. But could she? Her husband had left the house. Night was not something outside of her.

She heard her father's voice over her mother's. There would be pine pitch on the sleeve of her overcoat. Her father would send her back out to fetch turpentine from his woodshop. She would linger there even in the dark, run her bare hand along the newly finished surface of a commissioned piece of furniture. Smoother than anything in real life. Then facing the house with the kitchen aglow she would catch the first drifters in the halo of frayed light. For a moment or two such snowflakes would be countable and for that moment it would seem absolutely necessary to herald each and every one of them as single threads cut loose from a thick sky of unnameable color.

Inside, she would pivot around the tacky sleeve of the long woolen coat while her father dabbed at it with turpentine; the tenor of women's work, she could tell by his awkwardness, big hands working with reverence but little poise.

They would ask each other: will it snow tonight? Meaning not a gentle sifting, not some kind of confectionary dusting, not that which could be done away with by a good stiff broom; but the kind of snow that made you tunnel. That hid the ground till April.

If the night snaked out forever she could always get up to work on her collages.

The snow would snuff out the night and the joists and beams that supported the house, this very same house, oak and maple, tapered like hand-dipped candles, were calm from the center. The same slanted floor, twenty-inch boards in some places and pine, soft and dented.

We'll have to wait till the moon comes up, her father would say.

Why will we have to wait till the moon comes up? her small brother would ask.

To see if it's a snow moon, said her father. It would echo. To see if it's a snow moon, a snow moon.

With Sarah Leary she carved letters into birch trees. You just needed an old nail. Pierced the bark like skin. You could always find a nail in your pocket. Birches grew in groves as if to protect themselves. With Sarah Leary or Abigail Joslin she cleared the forest floor down to the sheen of another year's leaf matter, placed stones in a ring. You were rich if you found quartz.

She would close her eyes. Her palms flat down on bared ground. She could feel the tree humming.

By now her husband would have reached the Giddens farmhouse. She knew how the girl Frances was shamed by the molting, the softness of her new body. Last spring she had bloomed earlier than witch hazel. As if her skin put out a thick oil. Her hair held minerals and became coarse. Beauty shifts its weight, thought Mrs. Heald, to lean harder upon new places, to bruise the places it uses as footholds, to leave tracks across hips and behind the knees.

Willard had never cared for beauty. But here a girl had bloomed earlier than witch hazel, with a fur as fine and soft as pussy willow, felted nubs on magic wands. Mrs. Heald could have followed her through the forest blindfolded for her green and fishy scent.

She could stand it no longer. It was warm enough to go out in her nightgown. The White Pine shifted and creaked. Her father and her brothers shucking out the saplings that came up beneath the White Pine's skirts. Vitreous needles, like wind chimes.

If she went swiftly she could still find him out in the open. If she waited he would have gone for cover.

Past the place that would be known as the Abbott-Bickley house if the latter could just stick for one winter. The road porous and more stony than in the morning.

Past the apple orchards that quilted the downhill side of the Giddens property. Even through July's vast leafiness, those ruthless angles. All summer, she thought, fickle fruit hard as knuckles until suddenly, when everything else in the garden was turning under, they bore—sweet and red.

She felt a shiver. What if he were stationed beneath the child's bedroom window.

No, she forced herself onward. She had not those sordid visions. She was made of some very solid material. Granite washed down, hammered and split and forged an ice age ago.

Her husband was made of fabric and paper and wings. She would not go looking. She would simply stand in the yard and call to him.

The Giddens house was still lit from shoulder to shoulder. She hadn't noticed the clock as she left her bedroom. She was in nightgown and Willard's low boots. The young woman boarder she had noticed before sat on the bench in the lilac smoking. Inside the revelers were still drinking tea and she caught glinting flasks and tumblers. Their voices carried out over the lawn and across the road to the old woman in shadow.

Presently a couple spilled out the door and joined the young woman in the lilac. Through the topaz window she saw Frances Giddens emerge from the kitchen with a tray of refreshments. Surely it was Robert Yates who rose to meet her. As Vivian had said, she could feel the girl tremble. He took some morsel from the tray and nodded a gracious thank you. Frances turned back toward the kitchen. The young man followed her. Frances quickened her step and he after her.

They did not reemerge in the lighted parlor.

"Mrs. Heald," he said quietly when she had closed the door behind her. "You'll catch a chill in your night-clothes."

She turned on the electric. He was fully dressed, even his old cap on.

"I've been up to Abbott's," he continued with great calm. "Talked to Hal Bickley."

"At such an hour?" By force of habit her composure returned in the presence of her husband.

"Indeed. City folk know no darkness. Their streets are stunned beneath perpetual illumination."

"I had gone after you to Giddens."

"Ah. The summer boarders are throwing an orgy."

"Willard!"

"Then we'll return to slumber. But I thought you should know I've struck a bet with Bickley."

"You're not a gambling man."

"I am when it's the other man's currency."

There was a light pause—as if he had already lived this moment.

"And when there's nothing for me to lose. If he makes it to the first snow we're even. If he leaves before November well then the Abbott Farm comes to Willard."

⚜

(First snow took the forest into its body like a caterpillar or an angel. Took the road and the houses made squat by its drifting; the lone one on a slope, fearful, righteous spinster or Tory. A hard frost didn't consume more than tomatoes. First snow defaced, then assumed things mysteriously. A dooryard went blank. A graveyard lost all sense of sorrow. Apple trees their angles.

(Mrs. Heald stood helpless, accomplice to snow by birth.

(As a child she would open her mouth wide for the snow to rush in. Air that no longer tasted like apples, or earth. Her head chimed in this air, her tongue tasted rank and fleshy by contrast.

(Ice crystals would form where her hands sweated through her mittens. She knew even then that those who lived by the weather survived the winter.

(The White Pine did not lose its verdure in winter but grew thicker, as an animal who acquires a fine furred underlayer against the snow.

(This was something Willard knew also.)

But what if by some feat (they were young; or by craft) the new residents saw through the winter? What if it were his own wife who helped them? He remembered when they were married ("Forty years ago," he tried) it was a joke with friends, townsfolk, that for all he was dour, she was blithe. Of course her cheer had faded, and his somber aspect—well, witness his light demeanor with Frances!—but she still had enough warmth to share with Vivian Bickley.

(Then he thought: How well I am known to myself. For example, warmth is something I've never needed. I've the same light cap through all four seasons.)

He had done Abbott a turn and now Abbott could be of use to him. The postman hadn't enjoyed framing a new house. The men had decided not to dig a cellar but to lay the foundation across granite blocks in a new-fangled manner.

The first time he paid Abbott a visit the man was home and they stood outside the house for a time and Abbott showed him where a skunk had already lodged herself between the granite blocks and Abbott's floorboards. As Willard was halfway down the road Abbott caught him (could you imagine Abbott running? Willard nearly laughed aloud. The hermit's strides long and silent) and blurted, "Have they changed it much, the old homestead?"

"You're a great sentimentalist after all, Abbott."

If Abbott was hurt by the remark he didn't show it. His face was like an old Indian Head. (Then Willard regretted what was surely rudeness. It came to him like this: the two boys, maybe joined by another, had placed pennies on the tracks that cut a tiny corner off of Garner's rough triangularity. In the first weeks of this pursuit the flattened coins were the most coveted item of trade. Then when the storekeepers wouldn't take them, first Abbott, then the others realized the shiny disks were worthless.)

The second time the postman visited Abbott's he could tell a quarter of a mile away the place was empty. He'd had an inkling Abbott would be gone to town—it was Heald himself told Abbott about a truckload of chicken feed directly from the Maynard station—the manufacturer was giving it away as a guarantee your chickens would grow that much fatter.

(Abbott was down to chickens with their fast-beating hearts and tender liver and, as the last residue of a farming life he had elevated their station and gave them much foolish attention.)

You didn't need a gun if all you had were fowl—and Heald knew for a fact Abbott wouldn't shoot a fox before he'd coaxed it out of the thicket to keep him company. There was the broom Mrs. Heald had lent him and the shotgun. Side by side, Heald wondered. He was glad it was already loaded because it was one thing to borrow a man's weapon and another to ready it. The butt of it stuck out of his mailbag but it was only a short way to Bickley's. There was no question: he would plant it in the foaling shed.

⊱•⊰

It was not till the end of the summer that Frank Abbott returned to the old homestead, his birthplace. Vivian Bickley had found roadside asters: luminous sapphire with the sunrise, warmed to purple at midday, and ice blue by evening. She reached for branches of early-reddened swamp maple, tearing a damp pale swath down the whole trunk, to display in Japanese painted vases about the unfinished house.

There was a sudden, early frost. Vivian's token tomatoes lost their matte finish and their firm. The skin looked waterlogged, the flesh pithy. When Frances Giddens came with eggs and milk Vivian showed her one of the ruined fruits with horror. "The taste," she said, almost ashamed.

"And the texture is like that of your own tongue," Frances finished for her.

Heald noticed the way their cast-iron stove burned fast and hot. He figured the way Hal had installed it—with both ignorance and impatience. He withheld his estimate of how many cords of wood it would eat in a winter.

In the woods, Heald watched them tromping down an entire fern colony, sliding toward the pebbled streambed. The sound of their footsteps was earsplitting, but when Vivian, tanned to umber, confessed to him she daydreamed of moccasins he coldly retorted, "Why do all newcomers love the Red Indian?"

He saw that a city woman in the country got slimmer while a country woman of reasonable health in her native rural (as his wife) thickened. He saw that Vivian was contented when she left his wife's kitchen and his wife in turn was milder and sometimes distracted. He had heard the drone of Mrs. Heald's voice go on a whole morning. When he got close to listen he found it mesmerizing but unintelligible.

He noticed that the Bickleys often went their separate ways in the late afternoon; so that they might reconvene for supper. Vivian wandered, pacific, down Abbott Road as if she owned it and Hal (for in his head Willard was on familiar terms with them) stayed around the place, always ready to strike up a torrent of unwanted banter with whomever he had employed for his carpentry. Most of the men disliked working on the old Abbott farmhouse—Heald had seen a couple of lads who were all the way from Westborough or Saskoba.

Vivian, for all her ruddy complexion, would be the daydreaming type. Her letters were unduly long: meandering logic and a child's candor regarding her fears. Heald surmised she was left-handed. She wrote to women friends about her husband—as if there were not the same pact between them that Heald shared with his wife—the deep silence of loyalty. Well, she was afraid of the coming cold winter and of her husband injuring himself while performing that "rather barbaric and carnal act: wood splitting."

Heald traced her steps. In another letter she wrote, "We are pioneers, here, Gladys! Clover in the lawn just as in the dreams of childhood." Heald knew that life rested lightly upon her shoulders.

It was late afternoon when he detained Vivian along the road. (Moccasins, Willard spat with contempt.) He had seen Abbott glide through the woods, seen by the shadow, Abbott had grown a beard.

It pleased him to see she was surprised he wanted to walk with her. Many times before he had afforded only a curt nod if he had not broken off before they made eye contact. He had not considered that he would have to converse, cite a reason for his escort.

"A woman should not be walking alone," he said wrongly.

Sometimes she seemed gangly like a boy to him; other times a breathtakingly foreign idol. A dark doll, a red-lipped flower. How he longed to make her know he had caught her at the fraud of posing as a local.

"But walking on my own property, Mr. Heald?" she said almost coyly.

It was true that both sides of the road were Bickley forest. But the woman walked upon the road. In well-heeled shoes since she had no moccasins. Well they could argue then. His mission was to detain her and just by his escort to strip her of some propriety.

The postman felt his heart rising as he and Vivian Bickley approached the farmstead. The ring of the axe had long since ceased so that Heald knew how much time the two men had already passed together. Vivian hadn't noticed the quiet but had kept up her end of the light argument. (She believed that her land would turn a great profit, for quiet places were scarce and now people could take their education with them. "Pardon me?" said Heald in genuine confusion.

("Well we're highly entertained by the likes of you, Mr. Heald," teased Vivian Bickley. Willard felt distracted. He had his own concerns.)

Bickley would think Abbott had been drinking to come on strong, he thought, even crazed like a beast out of its element. But Heald knew that time was a Garner man's liquor—long, quiet solitude—the power to wait out any other man in the world. Heald knew: Abbott had been lurching about his new house through the clear-skied nights of early autumn. Bug-eyed, fish lips, crying. Heald felt an unreasonable dispassion. Frank Abbott with a mawing disease in his chest. Frank Abbott who had lived as a hermit, slept beneath the boughs of a pine lashed together with lightly pilfered hemp line. The rope out of Heald's milking room. "Now Mrs. Bickley," he interrupted her ever so calmly. "It looks as if your husband has company."

(And yet he had written for his record; and seen all the men in Abbott, the fortresses and lean-tos of cut brush they built as boys . . .

> (In defense of Franklin Abbott, not a sill survived. He fed two cows to the fire, his dog, Margaret's tightly braided carpets. All the men by the stove in the store share the same memories: the state of the father's teeth, the mother's everlasting leanness. Thin as a man is thin, buried deep on the property.)

The yard would look to Abbott strangely clean and innocent. He would feel the difference in the light— they'd cut out the dead trunk of the maple. He would pick up a rock against a dog curled alongside the house. He would nod to Bickley and stride past him. Heald knew Abbott had only ever shot to kill a burgling crow, a ewe bled out in hard labor.

Or, the gentle hermit struck to his knees by the sound of the axe, the splitting of hardwood, even pinewood. His heart would have surged. It could as well have been his mother—such an easy grace—he used to watch her, lithe, boyish.

There was the Bickley dog with its nasal barking. Heald led Vivian into the dooryard.

Abbott would remember when, as a boy, he had shot his own mutt in the leg before he could think not to. The way a boy is when a father hands him a gun for the first time, Heald thought now. The dog had crawled beneath the barn and bled to death and old Mr. Abbott who was Franklin too would have had to tear the barn down to retrieve him. Never seen a dog with so much pride, the men at the store said. The boy Franklin told the boy Willard, "A ginger cat ran away from the smell of it," as corroboration.

(It would be the very same shotgun. It was a wonder it had taken Abbott so long to find it gone missing. The lout Bickley. Who would steal a man's gun after already taking his farm? Willard imagined as if thinking for Frank Abbott.)

The dooryard was merely an opening in the woods and caught in a shard of light. Vivian called out to her husband, gaily, and Heald felt a blush spread up his neck and jowls.

It was as it should be. Hal Bickley and Frank Abbott stood facing. The moment was held up, twirled for weight and luster. Bickley had not dropped the axe in surprise. Heald caught Vivian's arm as she lunged toward her husband. He had not wanted to look at her for she was friend to his wife and doubtless her face would be contorted. But it was hard to keep a good grasp on someone without looking. Her face was of potash and drawn back as if she rode an open train car at a great speed. Her mouth gaped but no sound issued. He had not wanted to see some great ugliness but this was worse: a warm and innocent mammal. So she loved her husband. Well he would fling such love from a brutal height so that nothing of its body would reach the earth.

It seemed to Willard that Abbott lowered the gun serenely. Then it was as if out of such a crystalline blue sky (because the sky was clear, Willard thought later) came Abbott's familiar voice. "Was missing my gun was all," he said. "Good day to you, Heald."

Part Five
Garner

I

Could Frances say she was flattered by Miss Nillsen's attachment? Certainly vanity was to be shunted. Miss Nillsen begged Frances to call her Malin. Frances refused to seal a friendship. They went about the house together— Frances even fashioned a second duster from peacocks' feathers.

("Mr. Herman, I've a purchase to make of my own money but it's not from your store." She would have paused like a cat with raised paw: "A purchase from your barnyard."

("A peacock duster, Miss Giddens? What fine lady have you recently employed as maid?"

("It's not for me, to be sure, and only an indulgence for one of our boarders."

("Is this a business I should consider? Will there be further demand for such household accessories?"

("I'd be so much obliged if you'd name your price, Mr. Herman. Keep in mind that I am an excellent collector of peacock feathers.")

Miss Nillsen petitioned to be taken on excursions through the woods but Frances rarely consented. The city girl was too lovely for the woods—Frances preferred to be alone—and, she laughed, "The trees shouldn't like you as competition."

Miss Nillsen did not seem to be troubled by what course she should take in life—or perhaps it was that she was already in such a life that for Frances bent beyond the woods, illusory. But Frances had stopped waiting for her letters. Miss Nillsen was a live letter, blazing correspondence from a far world.

She allowed herself: it was strange—was it exhilarating?—to have that other world so evidently needful of her.

And then she quit writing out her thoughts (and a few wan or amputee stories) because she knew that if Miss Nillsen should ever come upon the pages, she would probe them to their depths and assign truths to Frances's character that Frances herself had not yet discovered.

Oh, Miss Nillsen was pleased with the feather duster. She went about like an actress on film. She was taller than Frances, hair like cornsilk—hair like first snow—most likely the queen of her country.

Frances's mother said they resembled each other as sisters do but Frances knew better. Frances's chest was a tin washboard, her stomach a furrowed pit. Miss Nillsen was in flower. Miss Nillsen said, "Frances, your hands are like irises."

Frances made two fists and would not open them until she was locked in private. Then, saw only the pale spiders.

But she hadn't an aversion to taking Miss Nillsen through the orchards. Such trees were allegiant only to the farmer. Here they might walk side by side or break into a run that invariably put them both in fine humor.

"Young ladies don't run, Frances!" Miss Nillsen called. "What on earth will become of you!" Frances felt her lungs swell, her forehead pound as if she were on horseback.

Miss Nillsen was a great one for producing tidbits of food at any moment. They might drop down beneath an apple tree and out of nowhere Miss Nillsen had filched a boiled egg and biscuit. A sack of slightly squashed raspberries would come tumbling out upon her skirts. Frances wondered at how this odd meal produced not only a sudden hunger but a warm enclosure, not a mere room but a chamber, where once had been only orchard grasses, deer tracks down the ditches. Well, old Giddens bread was transformed by Miss Nillsen into a picnic.

Frances said pines were once six feet in diameter. "Can you imagine such a forest, Miss Nillsen?" Her eyes shone. "Do you recall your arithmetic?"

"Circumference is one thing, height another matter entirely," said Miss Nillsen gaily.

"Taller by a barn's height than the Garner steeple." She laughed. "Oh, no. Then ten times as tall."

"You'd make fine company in a barroom. How did they ever chop such trees down?"

"By girdling," said Frances with solemnity. "You'll find Garner men who do it still. A belt around the trunk a foot deep."

"Corpulent ladies!" laughed Miss Nillsen.

"The soil has lost richness," said Frances. "Or folk have lost patience."

She showed Miss Nillsen the stone arch bridge where Abbott Road crossed over Blood Brook. Miss Nillsen skidded down the bank. The water smelled as clouds should smell and "Look up," commanded Frances. "You might have been in Revolutionary times beneath such an archway."

Miss Nillsen implored her for landmarks and Frances saw how the city girl was determined to make an internal language of the unmarked dirt roads, woods that barely breathed a path between beech grove and stand of hemlock.

"There is a covered bridge that has a life of its own," Frances said before she could keep such a secret.

"It happens just so," she went on, nearly breathless. "You've played the weather like a professional gambling man. You've waited ten days in June for the day to cut, and ten days to dry in the field. Raked it twice and bound it against mold and rodents. You've called half the town to heave bales. The old men and boys to stack them.

"You're pulling a teetering load from the Heald field down Abbott Road to Temple's and up comes a fully whiskered-and-bearded June thunderhead.

"No one thinks about money, Miss Nillsen. Not even Mr. Heald whose hay it is, or Mr. Temple, whose sheep will have it. But this is the crop that makes us civilized people! Our ancestors cleared the forest. We have milk and butter instead of roots and berries. Someone shouts from the hayride, 'Save the hay, you! Up ahead, the covered bridge down that turn-off!'

"The load tips dangerously with the turn and the boys atop call Whoa. But the tall wagon makes the grassy track before a raindrop has fallen, and you get-up the horses and pull under the covered bridge and the boys clamor down the bank to whittle sticks beneath it.

"Have you ever bared your head to a summer rain, Miss Nillsen?"

After such a stolen meal, Miss Nillsen would turn over and lie upon her half-full stomach. She braided grass stems into miniature wreathes and tied them about her fingers. Frances might have taken off her shoes had she been alone but she couldn't bear the intimacy Miss Nillsen would assume and she fell quiet instead. The sweet green metal smell of pine at the edge of the orchard. Or amber.

More than once she saw someone pass among those pines, a sack thumping against his sore back. Miss Nillsen saw him a moment later and she was up and racing through the orchard. Frances understood her impulse. Silver flame in the wake. As if the pursuit were taking place across her own body.

Miss Nillsen walked back to Frances slowly. A bank of chill air. It was getting late. Old leaves rotting, the perspiration of the forest. "You see, Miss Nillsen, how the ground at dusk shall drop out from underneath us."

It surprised her that Miss Nillsen liked to be out in dusk as she did. A beech might burst into silver flame. Then it would be darker than before and only the sharp acrid smell remained. Her heart lurched—sunk its blunt heart-teeth into a soft spongy spot at the base of her throat.

Miss Nillsen detained her, took her by the arm, matched her face so that Frances was compelled to listen. "You do so resist a laugh, a bit of leisure. Where are you off to and why can't I join you?"

Frances changed her course—not that she was meeting anyone in particular, but that she was dreaming of him—and alighted through the forest, down the stream bank. She shed her shoes before Miss Nillsen caught up to her. She waded out to a sandbar, called, "Beware! The stream tickles behind your knees, Miss Nillsen!"

"Well Frances, you play the part of a wood sprite exquisitely."

"You'll write volumes of poetry," called Miss Nillsen. "I see it now, letters like droplets of water, a word for each pebble."

"You're a fortune-teller, Miss Nillsen."

"Indeed," Miss Nillsen went on, "if you won't show me your palm, I'll read your lovely eyes, Frances. There shall be a young man, too; help me here: dark or fair? A city man or a farmer?"

Secrets, Frances put down despite her pledge to quit the diary, are the shadows of the plain truth between us.

There was a ghost who drank from the stream the way a bird drinks.

Owl:

By the edge with none to witness.

Swallow:

Not at home in the forest. Swoops in and skims the surface without ruffling the water.

There were midnights now she woke like a torch, ignited. Her dreams were in violation of that strict code of girlhood. For it was the gentleman Robert Yates—a city man, not a farmer. Her stomach tasted like something from an empty bowl and she swallowed, leaned out of the narrow bed to save the washing. Her body was sharp so that her own hands recoiled.

Would he be at the door now or later?

Outside in the dark, the clapboard farmhouse seemed to crouch peevishly against the wide banner of stars. Miss Nillsen had asked her, "When you are hidden away in your muted forest, Frances, is there someone you wish to find you? Someone who would uncover your face of fern and bracken?"

She hadn't responded. She was stranded on a slick gray rock midstream and Malin Nillsen had a sure foothold in the veiny, exposed roots that made a lace of the shallow water. But now, woken at this flimsy hour before the sunrise; the old trees in the Giddens yard as lifeless as tooth, stake, plinth, or pillar—she might answer the provocations of the city girl:

"Women used to be killed for such," she would say. "Women that wanted men were witches."

Frances picked up a stick and flung it.

"How were they killed, such women?" Miss Nillsen would insist.

"Hung," she replied.

Dogs
Stones
In the cool underside of morning.

"Tell me about stones," Miss Nillsen would keep up her prodding.

"I shall tell you of coyotes," Frances replied. "They were chased up the mountain past the tree line to bare rock. The men circled and stoned them. Bounty men had got all the wolves already."

⌇•⌇

Then mist began to rise from the rose-colored earth. The windows of the farmhouse glowed around the edges. The same trees recovered from dust to green. The body heat of the trees, and the mist began dripping.

("By law," she had told Miss Nillsen, "one is not permitted to pluck the lady's slipper flower that grows more rarely each year in our woodland acres. But I should like a dress fashioned of its skin."

(Delicate pouch, she thought. Endangered organ.)

In a moment her mother would cross the yard to the henhouse. To no one else would she bequeath that ritual of morning. Frances remembered her mother's words from childhood: "A bright alcove on one side of your heart, the stable of the sun, that is our God, Frances."

The kitchen was now flooded with light. Mrs. Giddens stood in that bright alcove with flour like a salty cloud around her. She clapped her hands to see Frances and the cloud exploded with a clean, hearth smell.

Miss Nillsen would not yet be awake.

The others, Robert Yates, would sleep practically until noon.

She knew now for certain she might commit an act so reprehensible, so entirely physical. It was her mother's presence, her mother's innocence that caused a well of disgust to rise. With her fist in her gut she bolted.

Robert Yates found her in the orchard. She had tamped down a path in the rich salad of grasses and surely enough he had followed with little effort.

"It seems quite impossible to imagine another season," he said when he saw her.

"Certain birds," she replied, "stay awake all through the night in summer." Not the hawk but if he were a bird he would be one.

Broad-wing hawk or sharp-shinned hawk—both follow the coyote.

Frances squinted up to watch one circling high above the orchard.

"What a great languor of weather," said Robert Yates smoothly.

"You city folk are eloquent but I know my ducks with their swivel necks and fine posture."

"Ah," said Robert Yates. "You shall narrate for me the difference between the wood duck, black duck, hooded merganser."

How was it that he was familiar in any language? Even the sheen of bill and headfeathers—he had shown he was an apt learner—the mulchy water of the beaver pond still on his boots from their last meeting.

He was keen to know all the native flora. "No, Mr. Yates," she repeated, a scarce smile, "there are no roses till July's bitter ending.

"Laurel is the Garner rose," she added.

Its frivolous blush deceptive for it had no pretty scent and its sturdy flesh boasted a long and indiscriminate middle age like an unmarried woman.

"There is no season in New Hampshire without something to endure, is there," said Robert.

Why did he say such a thing? Was he sorry for her; did he offer some rescue from the harsh calendar? Or did he make a simple observation? Frances had never considered it an endurance—the wait for roses. But he was right again. No season was better than the other.

"And of our birdlife? What else do you wish to learn? In the orchard our year-round residents are nuthatches; both hairy and downy woodpeckers."

They did not walk, customarily, through the woods together as she did when coerced by Miss Nillsen, but he managed to find her in the orchard, some undesignated hollow along the course of Blood Brook. She made certain that when waiting (for she had not before in her life had any reason to be waiting) her hands were carefully composed, even at her sides. Otherwise, she might put her palm to the ground, her ear in pine needles, to listen for the dissenting voice of Garner.

Where before she had always looked out for Mr. Heald the postman, she now deftly avoided his shadow. Of course, she told herself, she had ceased to care for her letters, but his company, too, which used to amuse her, seemed now of the most redundant order. More than once she spied him at an unpoised distance and she looked away quickly, the sky suddenly low and flat as a tin plate. The light bald and lemon-yellow.

She could tell that Mr. Yates had not seen him.

At home, Frances and Mr. Yates barely noticed each other. Once she saved a choice morsel for him but caught herself before she could bend to serve it. The platter was hot in her hands and she had to put it down upon the table. Miss Nillsen jumped up and took over in unsolicited loyalty.

It was a lunch and afterwards she fled the kitchen and out toward the dark fringe of woods that finally tilted down the bank to the water. She paused there—an old globe of red clover caught on the sleeve of her sweater.

It calmed her to walk downstream, then, jumping rocks and muffled roots, shoes long abandoned. She pulled back the striped maple saplings that encroached and they made a twang like bows stretched for ancient arrows. Or moosewood, she could advise Robert, for the moose with the itch upon his side who striped it.

The stream widened and the bank flattened out to make a lane of sand along the edge. An inland beach— New Hampshire needless of seashore, distant horizons. Just ahead, the covered bridge spanned the stream at its broadest.

She walked back and forth carefully, testing the boards. She would remember to tell her father that one or two would be soon rotting.

The light fell, or lifted. She had never considered such a thing: where did the light depart to as it made way for rain, great clods of thunder?

Her longing was terrible and it astounded her.

She began to dread her rambles with Miss Nillsen. Only when she was alone could she fully conjure him.

She felt burdened with his admission; the casualness with which he had said, "Ah, Malin and I were never meant for each other." Would she ever be able to claim it in the positive? "Meant for"—to summon such a declaration? She thought Miss Nillsen was unaware she and her fiancé had come uncoupled. Miss Nillsen never spoke of Robert. She seemed intent on learning something from Frances and, when on more than one occasion Frances had said shortly,

"But I've nothing more to show you, Miss Nillsen," she replied sadly,

"The country life is so sweet, Frances. I want to drink in all of it.

"And I have a frightful feeling you won't come back with me. That you're quite immune to my generosity.

"I thought this summer to be skipping over all of the Continent but here I've found a real friend and her lovely countryside."

She conceded to call him by his Christian name but she never spoke of her emotion. Only this: "Robert, you've come a far distance to find me."

He touched her shoulder briefly and motioned for her silence.

The wind a fine-feathered embrace. Instead she felt for the first time lonely.

The Maynard Pit looked to her like the old eye socket of an animal skeleton. She followed him away from it through the forest. How was it that he knew the way to skirt it and find the road at a point much closer to Garner?

At the juncture of road and forest he turned to her and helped her over the muddy trench. She might have rushed toward him.

But when he broke their long silence he said, "We've so little in common, Frances."

In the middle of August, Miss Nillsen unexpectedly departed. Although Frances's father protested, she paid him for the remaining weeks of the summer. Frances's brother Wright said it was a great boon and she was ashamed for him and called Miss Nillsen graceful.

She rounded up some industrious children for berry picking and made dense pies and ice cream for Miss Nillsen's farewell. Her mother was dejected but Frances felt some animal relief that she neither shunned nor welcomed.

II

Mrs. Heald was waiting for it come autumn.

A husband only makes one great confession to his wife in a lifetime and her husband had made it. In the way of the Puritan descendant: not outright said it. But over two seasons left a tortuous and exacting road map.

Spring he had been out every night walking. Past the time for snowdrops, crocuses, past the return of birds, past the thaw that cracked fire ponds and cow ponds and duck ponds making a clean start on every farmstead in Garner.

At first, he said other men were out too with the syrup. "But those men you call horses," she replied softly.

Since he had told her once that he would go out walking at night, he did not have to tell her again and shortly he stopped making excuses.

"You aren't worse for the wear, Willard," she said once in an attempt to gain his confidence.

"It wasn't the collapse of the china cabinet," she said when he looked up startled. Only your old wife, her soft voice like a slipper.

Summer she knew their paths crossed without planning. Everyone was out in summer. She herself, taking the new neighbor for mushrooms.

In September Mrs. Heald heard the girl might go away with the boarders. Vivian Bickley told her.

"I didn't know Frances was going away, then," she said to her husband, carefully.

"She'd had it in her mind to."

"She hopes to marry?"

"She does not wish to marry."

"Are you still her confidante?" Her voice sharpened.

He was silent for a moment and Mrs. Heald could hardly bear to raise her eyes for the look in his weak, unwise owl eyes.

It was the change of seasons compelled him to walk at night.

"Too much time in those woods, Willard."

"Who says I go about through the trees and bracken? I'm a man of the roads, aren't I?"

"No," she said softly.

It was as if he were trying to send his laugh to her from a very great distance. He knew his wife could hear how wrong it sounded, warped even. But why should she decide suddenly he was a thief instead of a humble postman?

He had always grown restless at the quarter-marks of the year—here soft-bodied summer had heaved herself over and fall in full armor stood above like St. Michael and the dragon. The forest matted with tawny leaves, rust, a deep oily brown. The snow gods shook out their dusty blankets.

He had always wanted to get the last of the old and the first of the new.

The first frost came by night. Small warnings with bared incisors.

Or, just as you woke on a morning in March some green shoot would have found its way up before sunrise.

Night was the time when nature stole in.

His wife still stood glaring at him. "And what if it's not the woods I seek at all, dear wife, but the jolly town of Garner?"

It was meant for a joke—so that she might laugh and cover up his own false laughter.

He knew Frances's father was making charcoal. There had been a stir about it in town—some of the men in the store saying he should wait till October for it had been dry since mid-August. Killam from the Maynard fire squad was hanging about with a pound sack of nails for purchase and the men looked to him for guidance.

"Might as well make a bonfire in the hay," he snorted. "His second cut still on the ground."

"Temple's got his up two weeks ago and it's all north-facing."

Eben Temple could laugh at the poor siting of his farm in this company. His sheep were finer than anybody's.

"With three grown sons. Wright, James, Joseph."

"So's a bonfire we're expecting."

As his wife said, men like this were horses to Willard Heald, but he heard them anyway.

"Maybe as a kind of show for those city folk," someone suggested.

"Sure, and the city folk care only for their parlor games and Giddens's goose fat."

Frances's father was a hasty man, thought Heald. He headed toward Giddens'.

The postman got a draft of lithium spring water from Frances's mother. The preparations were in full swing. They'd hired a couple of boys to restack the wood tight down in the east pocket field.

"You'll heat with it come winter, then," said Heald. "A break from the splitting?"

"If it's cold as they say."

"I remember your husband's grandfather. The blacksmith."

"It's true Mr. Giddens wants to do some of his own iron work. Without the boarders around he'll need some occupation."

There was the same straight freckled nose. But her mother was a reddened country woman where Frances was a wood nymph.

"He charcoaled last year as well, Mr. Heald. We've a deep well and many hands. He even set our Frances up to keep the watch, was so easy."

"Frances?"

"She's wakeful. Wright says we'll put it to use. I've caught her out of the house before dawn on many a morning."

So it was to be a cold winter, another. Last winter he'd seen a moose on Abbott Road gone mad with hunger, stomping and biting the frozen ground. The moose charged young Asa Robinson in his father's motorcar and Asa braked and slid across the packed ice into a birch tree that should have broken, barely rooted as it was in run-off gravel. Heald had seen the boy's face at the frosty window. Hindquarters of the motorcar deep in the bank. The road was silent. The woods were silent. The moose leaned with his flank against the car. The fur-lidded eyes were half closed, he was tired. Asa banged on the window beneath the moose's oak-colored side. The moose lowered his head like a dog.

> Oak-colored, or might have been gold in
> the light, had there been that light; but it
> was a week before apple twigs were edible.
> Pussy willows like hairballs, curse the cat
> with her mouse in the dry barn.

> *—The circuit of a postman*

The motorcar would have quickly become cold. Asa hit his fist upon the window and still the postman did not reveal himself. The boy would have to get out and walk. But not with the moose there. "Shoo, shoo," Heald heard his muffled voice, reserved for fear of an animal.

It must have seemed to the boy Garner men arrived by miracle. Weston, who lived in Town, and Giddens, with a gun—Willard had never found out the reason.

> A moose gone mad with hunger who drops
> to his knees in the crusted snow beside a
> motorcar with a mere boy inside.

Peaceful Giddens shot the moose between his half-closed oak-colored eyes. The huge body fluttered and imaginary birds were set loose from between the ribs. A piece of the moose's antler broke off when his head hit the ground. Weston beat them to it, whined it was for his son.

The weight of the moose upon the earth was almost unbearable, Heald remembered.

> In such a season you dream of summer. Of overnight mushrooms, chanterelle, salamander orange. In winter the animals change color.
>
> Last year, the White Pine singled out a small red fox and whispered, Hunt by me. The fox hunted. A snowshoe rabbit who would've gone white. Had it been any other way, no one and no thing let on. Not even the salty quartz in the granite rockbed.
>
> —*W.H., Garner*

—⛥•⛥—

Some other noise must have already awoken her, for she was bolt upright; and he was certain of his soundless approach. The ground was damp, she offered the cot, and it was as if this warm hollow were her parlor and she a fine lady. "I cannot refuse," he stammered.

She was ever so much smaller up close than she had been even as an invisible bird in the branches. He was hot. Could hardly breathe through the smoke. He was burning her, he must be hurting her—but she kindled him as she turned her face toward his—

"You've come for my father and what a surprise to find me."

He must not let the forest swallow her again. Body of leaves and winking light.

His hand was burning her. His breath came out as fire. The old dog with charcoal in his teeth. He must keep her in Garner.

> Selectmen are required once a term to cir-
> cumnavigate the town of Garner. They don
> heavy socks of worsted wool and boots for
> marching through the forest.

She was gone before he could collect himself. Like lightning, the dog hurtling behind her. He fell forward in a long, slow arc; still reaching. Some piece of fabric was caught in his hand. So, it had been violent.

It seemed a folly of the universe, a mistake of reality, that the charcoal was still burning. That, like the dog, its warmth had not also followed her.

What had he done—chased her from her post. Now it would be her fault if a coal escaped and set fire across this tinder of a field all strewn with loose hay. He had seen it once before, and it was why the men at Maude's had been so quick to criticize Giddens: a ground fire that licked bare acres of cropland. Not a licking but a savage undressing. A fire that cauterized roots, turned topsoil to ash, stopped food for a generation.

Even if he found her she would never come back to him. He would not find her. She knew the woods better than he. Her young eyes like a cat's.

Not so much her father as the whole town would accuse her. He could drive her out himself. Even Buck Herman, sympathetic to all causes, who had before been called upon to settle matters of morality, would take Giddens aside: "She should go somewhere they've more than volunteer firemen, man. Let her go to New York City after the Swede. They had taken a fancy to each other."

"Let her play with fire elsewhere, Giddens," Tuttle of the sawmill would say. "Send her off with the red-haired gentleman."

There was no question in the postman's mind: Frances would not betray him. She had not the words to explain it. Even to her mother: "The postman visited me and I took fright."

"Fright of old Mr. Heald?" her mother would say in disbelief, maybe even some humor.

He rose. It was her due, he thought angrily. For playing with fire. And if he hadn't come the boarder would have found her.

The fire made a scuttling noise and he jumped back.

Let the Giddens field burn.

From the rise just above the charcoal pyre he could make out his own farmstead. Not yet a night for chimney smoke, but the cool slate roof gleamed in the moonlight like a shield. His wife was sleeping there.

He saw the field blaze. There was a way in which a ground fire looked like water. He had not seen the ocean but a windy lake provided the same heaves and whitecaps, he imagined. Which way was the wind blowing? He tipped his face heavenward. The fire would sweep east directly for his acres.

There was nothing to do but keep watch himself. He thought to wake up Giddens, but accusing the girl directly of abandoning the charcoal was out of character. He might go and get his wife for company. But even a trip of ten minutes was a risk he knew he was imprudent for giving consideration. Keep watch alone, Willard. He settled on the cot that had been made up tightly for Frances.

So, the girl will share a bed but not a forest, he thought as he spun into a slumber of bitter yearning.

In the early morning hours rain gathered and Willard slunk home and passed the time until the watery sunrise leaning heavily over the kitchen table. It was as if the charcoal-making brought the rain, his wife said later, and it was a rain like they'd not seen all summer.

When he awoke (face pressed upon that lame rabbit's foot that was Florida) Mrs. Heald had evidently been up to Abbott's-that-was-now-Bickley's. She was chopping and boiling and sizzling food not five feet away from him.

"A night of autumn air restores ten years to a man's heart," said Willard.

"And for a woman a morning stroll as they do for health in our nation's cities, says Vivian Bickley."

"It disgusts me, Mrs. Heald. The word 'stroll.' How shall you ever atone for such idleness?"

"By serving a man a solid breakfast."

"It's a hot stove, Mrs. Heald. You'll save some of that cordwood for October."

"Giddens is giving away charcoal," she hummed with pleasure. "Mrs. Bickley had not seen its making and we happened by the changing of the guard: father relieving his only daughter."

"Frances?"

So she had watched him from the woods then. Of course. He was wrong again. She would never have abandoned a fire. She had moved in as he left, despite the rain; a girl as Garner raised them.

⇥ III ⇤

A dream: earth an island of grass wearing a grass skirt. The view from the White Pine's leader: fault lines and the capricious curves of the Saskoba River. Fault lines and fields parceled off and marked in squares by slight variations in color.

The White Pine dreams not in years but in concentric circles.

There will be a year our stream shan't freeze over.

Yes, in places where it's shallow along the bank, thought Willard, platforms of white ice, but even a fox knows he can't step there. The White Pine laughs at us like she laughed at the caveman. If you think winter is long, consider history. Cousins of mine, says the White Pine, saw the dinosaur.

Your hands will chap and your brows become ledges.

One need not fear January. Even February has no pretense.

—W.H.

There had been a warm spell at the end of March. Five days, mushroom-like crocus up through the hay-mulch, white-stemmed, juicy.

"The White Pine has a great faith," called the girl Frances. From a White Pine, it seemed to him, although the sap should have prohibited climbing. "They choose it for Christmas."

> Roots send shivers to the leader on underground conduits of sap, a fountain inside a tree trunk. Maples become nursing mothers. Tracks sink in the sponge of leaves and needles on the forest floor. Paths emerge, the swaddling of wet snow disappears of its own accord. The White Pine tunes the instrument in her branches. Witch hazel the color of egg yolk, tangled forsythia in conference with the sun.

Willard recalled what he had said to the girl. "Five days of this. Out like a lamb, Miss Giddens."

She called, "Do you think the beeches that have split and lost branches forgive the ice storm?"

Sitting places dry out. Deer tracks on the muddy road. In the apple orchards, the soap that is hung in cloth bags to keep them away has been rainwashed to wafers.

At night, the wind picks up. The crown shivers.

A cat comes out—cat beneath whose step the crocus grows.

Toad dreams of Toad Lily, of Bleeding Heart, of Goat's Beard.

Houses are hovels. Maple syrup freezes in buckets, the old sugar house finds its voice.

The lights of an automobile wrack the forest.

There is an exact line in the air and on the ground where the headlights stop and the dark resumes. Anyone worth his salt knows this, Fox. White Snowshoe Rabbit doesn't know. The automobile shudders to a halt. The rabbit doubles back. Fox is waiting. Not even enough time for the death cry. Quiet in the woods.

Dead bellies turned over by the snout of another animal. Fur in the teeth. Pleading, we are only passing through. Mark us in the day, we are lost at night.

> Stars have their own might.
> No moon
> No need for moon
> March
> We are just passing through
> Rocks have their say: cold at birth
> Cold at death
> Stream goes black.
>
> The arch of night
>
> No song
> No death song
> The wind picks up.

—*Dreams Willard*

⊶ **IV** ⊷

(Then the sky lifts and the trees lift their jeweled branches and the world sparkles in the sunlight. Heald abandons his thick overcoat in a Joslin field as if it will never dry again so drenched with his own vile sweat, mushrooms under the arms, the weight of winter he will leave behind him.)

⊶•⊷

It was agreed that the remaining Giddens boarders would stay through September. No other farm still had boarders. There was more work in the month of September than all three summer months put together. Mrs. Giddens pleaded with her husband that it was enough for her and Frances without the cooking, serving, the linens . . . but Wright Giddens stepped in and said they must take a sideline and while it may have been neither dignified nor palatable it was what had presented itself. They would all work together; Asa Robinson could be hired by the day for some of the harvest, and there was a long winter of hibernation ahead of them.

Frances watched her mother closely. While Mrs. Giddens might have argued with her husband, she could not draw a word against her son.

There would be no more charcoal-watch for Frances— We can't afford the only daughter red-eyed in the morning.

Frances said nothing to this—felt nothing, strangely—she had done the job and would dwell upon the rest no further. Even when, later in that day or was it the next, Mrs. Heald paid a visit to Frances's mother and suggested since her husband was out all the night anyway he could be trusted and employed to keep the charcoal fire, Frances was as unmoved as the milk-cat.

The boarders seemed to go about their business as Frances attended to hers. There was little time for wandering through the woods and indeed Frances saw how this might be the year when she suddenly (and yet with no fanfare) slipped into her mother's skin. Became a woman, she forced herself to say it under her breath, and in her voice it sounded poor and defeated. She began to watch the boarders with envy. Not the flouncy young women who were her counterparts, contemporaries, but Robert Yates in particular. She burned with jealousy.

Because she no longer strayed from the homestead, they ceased their meetings. She understood now that her rightful place was in watching. In that way one might lead two lives at once. This helped to quell such envy.

It surprised her, then, when Mr. Yates strode toward her where she worked the farthest potatoes in the garden (once you dug a potato it would forever taste to you of the same dirt that dried your hands, smelled of absolutely nothing and of everything). They could not be seen from the house: just the same, she stood up properly.

"You've traded Diana for a real farmer's daughter," he said.

She made no response.

"It's not an insult, Frances. Only I'm sure you know your Septembers." He paused, looked her over quizzically. "It's more beautiful now in the forest than it was all summer."

"You're right, Mr. Yates. It's hardly an original discovery."

"Ah—I'll tell you what is, then, Frances. I've left my steel-toed cohorts behind and found an old covered bridge rather deep in the forest."

She laughed. Green and silver.

"You're laughing at me." He put his hand out and she did not recoil as she willed herself to. "Obviously no feature of the Garner landscape surprises you."

"No, Mr. Yates. I was born here."

"Still I'd like to show it to you. The bridge, I mean. It reminds me of you. A daring, and yet secreted, imagination. Would it please you to meet me there—this afternoon, early evening?"

"I shall be there on Saturday. Precisely at three. It's a work week we're just beginning."

Through the week it rained hard again and Frances maintained a stoop, an austerity so that he would not notice her. The time would come to stand tall and the contrast would cause him to take notice. She would not have the words to hold him away—and yet still she longed to see him framed by woods and yes, bridge, that place he had called secret.

Saturday the rain eased and her mother said, "Go, Frances, and do something pleasant. I can prepare a simple supper." As she knew her mother—so now she began to know herself.

She took the road and her walk became a swing; arms light as if from dancing. She felt the high canopy of leaves (were they new leaves? But it was September) arch above her. Beech, ash, oak, maple. She could hear the rush of the stream long before any city man's ears might detect it. The rush of it that had made islands and stranded trees and set rocks loose on its course. Her father had announced to the boarders: "It shall be full for the winter." Had proclaimed, quite innocently, "A glad and messy winter." There was soft air nesting on her shoulders. She was, of a sudden, the most beautiful creature in the woods. Her hair was light; her hair was wind. Around this corner, marked by a tree more guardian than the rest, the last indentation of an old pasture, master crabapple tree, hermit crabapple tree, she turned left onto the grassy track that led through a stand of beeches and finally down to Blood Brook, the bridge that spanned it.

Odd that it had taken a summer and more for him to find it. Of all the places in the woods, here was one still used, just last spring, for commerce. It seemed that he should have been able to sniff it out immediately. But she had witnessed: his way in the forest was to go blindly, then to borrow the magic of her resting places. Even the way out from the Maynard Pit—he had leaned upon her instinct.

The stream was swollen with autumnal rain, different from summer's fish-filled quenching cloudbursts, and Frances imagined it losing track of its rocks, smashing its careful pools into thoroughfares. This was what she came here for. If not for him, then to belong to such motion.

She would wait beneath the White Pine, its lowest branches amplifying wind in her ears, the overlay of many voices. Heat rose up her arms, her face; her eyes would tear from staring. I have come late to the crossroads of womanhood.

But it is not a crossroads after all, she laughed, it is a covered bridge. Would he appear from one side or the other?

Time rocked back on its heels. She stayed low and the tree whistled. An hour passed, then another. The forest began to settle itself after her intrusion—had slim regard for human conference.

Then she felt his presence behind her. Of course, he would have stood her ridicule if he waited on the bridge like a naked candle. I've been foolish, she thought as she turned about to meet him.

There stood the postman.

She startled gently but did not cry out. His eyes were so dry they cracked at the corners, white mouth, she knew: her limbs would flail and beat within the circle of their embrace and she would say neither yes nor no; was it what she had been waiting for, after all?

"Let us take cover," he said.
She followed so easily.

She was keenly aware of the stream below her. If only she might fall into it. In September, she thought with fear's lucidity, the stream is the haunt of old frogs who set up camp by evening.

She would not close her eyes. He found them once and closed his own in terror. His skin was hot and wet and prickled as if with some rash, poison sumac, poison ivy, the blisters of which would weep a yellow water.

Then there was silence; and stillness—no air to fill the sail. From far above came the familiar sound of Mr. Heald's step receding through the forest.

She moved down the bank like an old woman. Smell of green and blood and gingery fresh earth. Fragrant forest compost. Late afternoon like a wire pulled taut from tree to tree. White Pine lit from behind.

Robert Yates—the words held no meaning. Had there been the promise of a meeting, she had dreamed it. Well this, she knew, was the last girlish thought she would be privy to. If she had been gentled through a summer—what else to call it? For now she knew she could not call it romance—it was as fortune played you, with no love or hate or reason known to man or woman.

But now she was quite free of fortune.

She looked up into the cross-weave of branches and deep greenery.

So it was true. You had no choice in the matter. Took rocks with you as you rolled—but hardly a clatter.

⚜

What is in the stream, Willard? He squints as if at a reflection.

Far above the doctoring and the bickering of bird life in the autumn canopy a voice comes from the White Pine's leader: No place to rest. Not in your granite lap, Willard.

She is in the branches of beech trees, birds feasting on her ill-lit body. When she lets out her voice it is the sound of the White Pine's whistle.

Later, Buck Herman comes back with him. They lift the body out of the water.

Other men wait on the road. A sail-shaped shroud between them.

"Water in the lungs," says Buck Herman. Although the whole forest could smell blood in the water.

"Or one of those summer boarders."

She finds herself stuck in the high web of beech and ash and birch and farther out from the stream are the White Pine, oak, and maple. She notices how the leaves make little whimpering noises and she tears them off with her empty hands and the world is more green than was intended.

She is too light to do much harm. A dragonfly suggests arm wrestling. The mosquitoes gather and laugh when she loses. Their wings are made of mica and their bodies finely woven in shades of gray. The one more purple than the rest is their master with an easy malevolent whine and a sore shoulder.

Mr. Heald, she calls. There are secrets that bind you to your home.

The White Pine curries the winds but her hair is too light to be blown. It comes apart in still air and converses with late wings of pollen.

In the night she sits on a rock. Just before dawn she dreams of what must be love. The White Pine claims to know something of it. She closes her ears against it and she hears it through her heart. The heart of a ghost is tender and bitter like a dandelion shoot. She dreams of love and love hangs quietly in the air. If she drops it now, that kite, that bird, that soft floss of love into the rushing stream, the world would end. She keeps her ghost hands at her sides, thinking of Garner.

She knows now that the White Pine means no harm. Still she is jealous of the rule and vista. The White Pine says, I can see the road from here, who comes and goes, animals crossing. The White Pine says, Welcome, an exquisite word, round as a river stone. Passes it to her in feathery hands. In her mouth it is smooth and warm. She would spill the stones from her throat and rise even higher.

How they made the covered bridge: hammers and saws and loud laughter. A break for lunch in the woods. Somebody dug up an Indian cucumber and washed it clean and cold under water. Somebody else spied a jack-in-the-pulpit.

The first night is the longest. Then the dark lifts and a gray dawn curls like smoke underneath a bedroom door. Smoke becomes daylight.

Her laugh sounds like the stream to one not accustomed to hearing it.

Her laugh sets up a trembling through the forest although her body is only an indentation left from where eyes and heart were lodged. She is floating face up in a stream carved an ice age ago. She is staked through the stomach by a stone.

They use the wagon track. The White Pine watches. One man keeps talking. "This whole slope used to be pasture. Half potatoes and half cattle. In beetle season I could make a nickel for every hundred bugs I plunked in a can of kerosene."

Another man chimes in to cut the trembling as they approach the road and the White Pine lists in the wind to follow them. "I remember when this hillside was all apples. Northern Spies, Greenings, Porters, Pippins."

Buck Herman, who shoulders the weight of the girl, breaks in, "Sheep Nose, Early Rose, Pat Murphy, Irish Cobbler."

The engine starts up. The White Pine bears their dust and then the dust settles.

⇥•⇤

I had known that he would come for me. When they had taken my body up the bank my soul, with nowhere else to go, caught in the high branches of the beech tree. Gossamer.

I used history as a backdrop and catalyst for the drama that unfolds in Garner. Among many, the following three sources became touchstones for its imagined world.

J. C. Furnass's *The Americans, A Social History of the United States, 1587–1914* (New York: 1969) is a repository of rich, period language.

Henry Ames Blood's *The History of Temple, NH* (Boston: 1860) is an astoundingly lively amateur historian's love letter to his town. It provided a wealth of antiquated, colloquial names for trees, native fauna and flora, agricultural varietals.

I am indebted to *A History of Temple New Hampshire 1768–1976* (Dublin, NH: 1976, Editorial Committee, Anne D. Lunt, Ruth C. W. DeQuoy, William Nathaniel Banks, James L. Haddix, and Priscilla A. Weston) for its tireless recording of the rhythms and syntax of daily life in a small, southern-central New Hampshire town.

FUNDERS

Coffee House Press is an independent nonprofit literary publisher. Our books are made possible through the generous support of grants and gifts from many foundations, corporate giving programs, individuals, and through state and federal support. Coffee House Press receives general operating support from the Minnesota State Arts Board, through an appropriation by the Minnesota State Legislature and from the National Endowment for the Arts, a federal agency. Coffee House receives major funding from the McKnight Foundation, and from Target. Coffee House also receives significant support from: an anonymous donor; the Buuck Family Foundation; the Bush Foundation; the Patrick and Aimee Butler Family Foundation; Consortium Book Sales and Distribution; the Foundation for Contemporary Performance Arts; Stephen and Isabel Keating; the Outagamie Foundation; the Pacific Foundation of The Minneapolis Foundation; the law firm of Schwegman, Lundberg, Woessner & Kluth, P.A.; the James R. Thorpe Foundation; the Archie D. and Bertha H. Walker Foundation; West Group; the Woessner Freeman Family Foundation; and many other generous individual donors.

This activity is made possible in part by a grant from the Minnesota State Arts Board, through an appropriation by the Minnesota State Legislature and a grant from the National Endowment for the Arts.

MINNESOTA STATE ARTS BOARD

NATIONAL ENDOWMENT FOR THE ARTS

TARGET.

To you and our many readers across the country,
we send our thanks for your continuing support.

COLOPHON

Garner was designed at Coffee House Press
in the historic warehouse district of downtown Minneapolis.
The text is set in Perpetua.

Good books are brewing at coffeehousepress.org